TOUCH

FRANCINE PROSE

TOUCH

AN IMPRINT OF HARPERCOLLINSPUBLISHERS

HarperTeen is an imprint of HarperCollins Publishers.

Touch
Copyright © 2009 by Francine Prose

Library of Congress Cataloging-in-Publication Data
Prose, Francine.
   Touch / Francine Prose. — 1st ed.
        p.   cm.
   Summary: Ninth-grader Maisie's concepts of friend-
ship, loyalty, self-acceptance, and truth are tested to their
limit after a school bus incident with the three boys who
have been her best friends since early childhood.
   ISBN 978-0-06-137517-0 (trade bdg.) — ISBN 978-0-06-
137518-7 (lib. bdg.)
   [1. Coming of age—Fiction.   2. Best friends—
Fiction.   3. Friendship—Fiction.   4. Family problems—
Fiction.   5. Stepmothers—Fiction.   6. High schools—
Fiction.   7. Schools—Fiction.]   I. Title.
PZ7.P94347Tou 2009   2008020208
[Fic]—dc22   CIP
                                                 AC

Typography by Andrea Vandergrift
09   10   11   12   13   CG/RRDB   10   9   8   7   6   5   4   3   2   1
❖
First Edition

For Emilia

CHAPTER ONE

"Are the boys who assaulted you present in the court-room?"

"Your Honor, I object to counsel's use of the word *assault*."

"Objection sustained."

"Are the boys who *molested* you present in the court-room?"

"Objection, Your Honor. *Molested* is inflammatory."

"Sustained."

"Are the boys who *touched you inappropriately* on the school bus here today in the courtroom?"

I wait for the sputtery lawyer fight that will save me from having to answer. But this time, it doesn't happen. The courtroom is silent. No one moves. Someone coughs. Everyone's staring at me.

"Yes," I say.

"Can you identify the boys who touched you, Maisie?" I hate the way the lawyer speaks to me, as if I'm three years old, or as if I'll shatter in pieces if she speaks in the normal voice a normal person might use when that person happens to be talking to a halfway intelligent ninth grader.

I look over at the table where the three defendants sit jammed together with their lawyers. It's crazy that now they're *defendants*. Shakes and Chris and Kevin are my *friends*. Or anyway, they *used* to be my friends. When they were my friends, they wore baggy jeans and T-shirts and baseball caps. Now that they're defendants, they're wearing suits and ties and short haircuts. All three of them are hunched up tight so their shoulders won't touch their lawyers.

Chris and Kevin won't look at me. But Shakes and I make eye contact, or as much steady eye contact as you can make, considering Shakes has that funny twitch or tremor that keeps throwing him out of focus.

I'm trying to send Shakes a message. *I'm sorry. I can't help this. Please don't hold it against me.* But it's not getting through. Looking at him is like talking into a phone that you suddenly realize has gone dead.

"Will the witness answer the question, please?"

I try to speak. Nothing comes out.

And then, as always, my eyes blink open, and I wake up with the judge's voice echoing inside my head.

"So what do you think the dream means?" Doctor Atwood asks.

"I don't know." I shrug. It doesn't take a rocket scientist—or even a therapist, like Doctor Atwood—to figure out what the dream means, and to come to the logical conclusion that I'm pretending not to get it.

I look out the window. It's snowing. It may sound kind of egocentric, but sometimes I can't help thinking that lately the weather's been keyed in to my personal calendar. Every time I go to Doctor Atwood's office, it snows. It's only February, but already it seems like the longest winter in human history. In fact, it's a record breaker, the harshest winter in Pennsylvania history. I'm trying not to take it personally.

"Maisie," says Doctor Atwood. "Stay with the dream. What are you thinking? What does it mean?"

I'm thinking: *Is she kidding?*

My three best friends touched my breasts on the back of the school bus. Someone told the principal, and the whole thing kind of blew up. Now my family—my stepmother, Joan, mainly—is suing the school board for denying my right to an equal education. She wanted to charge my friends with sexual harassment or assault and battery or attempt to inflict emotional damage or whatever. Fortunately, her lawyer told her those cases are often harder to prove. Frankly, I was really relieved. As mad as I am at what my former best friends did to me, I still don't want to see them in jail.

Joan said, "These cases are all about he said, she said. And in your case, Maisie, it's he said, he said, he said, she said." Which was fine with me. Because there are all these different versions of the story of what happened on the bus. First I denied that anything happened, and then I told everyone that actually it was worse than what people were saying.

There's plenty to look at in Doctor Atwood's office, which is lucky because it saves me from having to stare back into her cocker spaniel eyes staring into mine. It's almost as if she wants to peer straight into my brain.

Half the time, I want to let her. Because the truth is, I'd be interested in knowing what's going on in there. The rest of the time, I'd prefer a little privacy.

So I look away and check out her collection of African statues and masks. I like to imagine that, every evening, after the last patient has gone home, Doctor Atwood takes the sculptures off the shelves and dresses them up like dolls. I imagine her ordering pizza or take-out Chinese food and feeding the masks as if they were babies, coaxing them to open their grinning mouths and jagged teeth, and take a tiny taste.

"Maisie?" she repeats, in her maddeningly calm voice. "Do you think the dream is trying to tell you something?"

"Do *you*?"

"There's no need to be hostile," she says. "I'm only trying to help. You know that, Maisie, don't you?"

"Actually, I do," I say. "So help me figure this out. My dad is paying you to keep me from being permanently damaged by my big traumatic experience. And to tell the court or the judge how crazy I am because of what happened on the bus. So if you're asking *me* what my dream means, my dad should be paying *me*."

"Maisie, I don't think you're crazy at all."

"I'm glad someone doesn't," I say.

"No one does," says Doctor Atwood.

"That's a comfort," I say.

"Just for the record," Doctor Atwood says, "I won't be testifying at any sort of hearing. I *will* write a report of some kind. But I want to promise you, I won't betray anything you tell me in the privacy of this office."

I say, "Like Las Vegas?"

"What?"

"Like what happens in Vegas stays in Vegas."

Doctor Atwood lets a minute pass. I look at a mask that seems to have blood dripping down its teeth. What a weird piece of art to have in a child psychologist's office. Oops. Doctor Atwood's lips are moving.

"What were you saying?" I ask. "Sorry."

She almost looks annoyed, then remembers she isn't supposed to. Probably the first lesson they teach you in psychotherapy school is don't look annoyed and act really interested even if you're completely bored.

She says, "You understand that your family thought it was a good idea if you started coming to see me. No one's forcing you—"

"I'm not angry." I mean it. I know that she's my expensive new paid best friend. But now that I no longer have any real friends, at least she's someone to talk to. "Maybe the dream is telling me that I'm nervous about the trial."

"Good," says Doctor Atwood. "Stay with that."

"Stay with what?"

"Your feelings about the trial."

"It's not a trial," I say. "It's a hearing."

"The hearing," she says. "I'm sorry. *Trial* was your word, Maisie."

"The hearing," I say.

"And your feelings about it are . . . ?"

"My feelings? I feel like total crap! I wish it wasn't happening. I wish it never got started."

I want to tell her how the whole mess often seems to me like one very long, very complicated bad dream, or like some evil chain email message that you don't take seriously, so you send it on to six friends, because it seems funny. And then each of your friends sends it on to six of their friends, and before you know it, the entire country is being told that they'll be run over by a freight train unless they send a dollar to a certain address. And finally someone breaks the chain and doesn't send the dollar. And that person gets run over by a freight train.

The reason I denied that anything happened at first was because the guys were my friends. And then I found out something totally insulting and gross. So I said: Okay. Fine. It happened. Then I said, Guess what? The incident on the back of the bus was *worse* than everyone thinks.

"And why do you think it *is* happening?" Doctor Atwood says.

"*It?*"

"The hearing. The case."

I say, "Ask *her*. It was all *her* idea."

"By *her* you mean your mom?" Doctor Atwood says. "Joan?"

"Joan is not my mom," I say. "Joan is the Wicked Stepmother."

"Should we talk about *that*?" asks Doctor Atwood.

Whenever we get anywhere near a Big Important Subject—and obviously Doctor Atwood thinks that my feelings about my stepmother are a Big Important Subject—she'll keep quiet and give me as much time as I need. Now I wonder if she'll give me so much time that I can get through the rest of the session without saying another word. I open my mouth and make little sputtering sounds, then close it again and frown as if I'm thinking really hard.

Doctor Atwood waits. I wait. More time goes by. My plan seems to be working. Because I hear a door open and shut, and sounds—throat clearings and assorted honkings and snorts—coming from the waiting room. The office is set up so that you enter through one door and leave through another, which means that you never have to meet the patients with appointments before and after you.

I've never met the guy who comes right after me,

but I have a name for him. Phlegm Man. Now, as always, Phlegm Man's revolting upper respiratory noises get louder and louder, as they do every time he's getting ready to see Doctor Atwood. Until they reach a crescendo, and it sounds like his sinuses are revving up to explode all over the waiting room.

"I think our time is up," I say.

Doctor Atwood looks at her watch. "So it is," she says. "All right. To be continued."

CHAPTER TWO

Leaving Doctor Atwood's office ejects me directly onto the snowy street. I look down at my sneakers and calculate how long it's going to take my feet to freeze. Then I turn around and tromp back into the building and upstairs to Joan's office. Joan is also a therapist, but only for adults. She knows Doctor Atwood, but not all that well. They're neighbors and colleagues, they say, and both of them have promised me that they won't discuss my case without my permission. *As if* I'd tell my therapist anything Joan shouldn't know!

I think, If Joan's still in her office she can give me a ride. But taped to the door is a Post-it that says, *Maisie! See you home. I heart you. Joan.*

It's just as well. So what if my feet get a little cold? The snow's almost stopped, the streets are hushed and peaceful, and I like walking past the pretty white houses and the pretty white lawns of our peaceful, half-suburban–half-country town. In fact I'm feeling pretty peaceful myself by the time I get home. But the calm instantly melts away in the steamy heat of our kitchen.

I don't want to seem paranoid, but I can't help wondering if Doctor Atwood could have called home and told Joan what I said about Joan not being my real mother. Because by the time I've walked back to our house at the other end of town, Joan's baking cookies. Cookies! Sometimes I feel as if Joan is constantly auditioning for a TV series being filmed inside her own head.

Today's show, on the Joan Channel, is entitled *Sitcom Mom*. Joan's wearing an apron and, around her hair, a scarf tied up in pointy rabbit ears. She's bustling around the kitchen, singing some million-year-old disco hit as she dumps chocolate chips into a bowl and smacks the batter around with a spoon.

"Maisie!" she says. "How was your session with Doctor Atwood?" Joan has one of those high-pitched voices that make you think the person has practiced sounding superfeminine and ultracheerful. It's less like human speech than the song of some annoying bird that wakes you up every morning.

I say, "The only reason I agreed to go to Doctor Atwood is because you and she made such a big deal about the fact that nothing I said there would ever leave her office. She would never tell you or Dad anything I told her. And now you're asking *me* what happened at our session? Isn't that sort of a contradiction?"

"I'm sorry," says Joan. "I respect that. As a professional, and a mother."

So now Joan's gone from Sitcom Mom to Doctor Joan Marbury, Therapist. Joan *should* have been an actress. That's what she does best. She loves playacting and dress-up. I think that's how she hooked my dad.

One afternoon, not long before I left Joan and Dad here in Pennsylvania and went to spend eighth grade in Wisconsin with my real mom and her new husband, Geoff, I went into my dad's—I mean my dad's and Joan's—bathroom. I'd run out of toilet paper and Sitcom Mom had forgotten to buy it.

Joan had washed her underwear and hung it over the tub to dry. It was all black lace and ribbons, the kind a stripper or hooker might wear. But definitely not Sitcom Mom or, for that matter, Doctor Joan Marbury, Therapist.

It grossed me out to think that she owned it, but I was *totally* grossed out by the idea of her wearing it, and even *more* totally grossed out by the fact that she would leave it out there like that, for anyone to see, in the house where she lived with two kids—me and Joan's own son, my stepbrother, Josh Darling. Also known as Darling Josh. His real name is Joshua Marbury, but Joan calls him Josh Darling this, Darling Josh that.

Since then, I've never been able to look at Joan without feeling as if I have X-ray—X-rated—vision that can see straight through her clothes to her underwear. Which, believe me, isn't something I'm eager to see.

Now she says, "You know that Alana and I don't talk about you. You have to trust us about that. But I can't help suspecting that you're probably not opening up to her yet."

Opening up? The words make me feel queasy, as if

I'm a patient on an operating table and Joan and Doctor Atwood are doing surgery on my brain. "If the two of you don't talk about me, how do you know whether I'm opening up?"

Joan flashes me a smile, dazzling me with fifty thousand dollars' worth of dental work, done for free by my dad.

"Maternal instinct, I guess," she says. "And professional experience. Maisie, dear, you always act as if you're trying to catch people in a lie. But the fact is, no one's lying to you."

If I live to be a thousand years old, I'll still never understand why my parents chose the people they married—remarried—after they split up. As far as I know, my dad's allergic to chocolate, so unless Joan's trying to kill him, which I don't think she is, you'd think she could bake oatmeal raisin bars. Or lemon squares. But if Joan can't do one thing right to help me get through this hideous time I'm going through, what makes me think she could bake cookies that anyone in our family might actually want to eat?

CHAPTER THREE

I was eight when my mom left. One day, she just packed up and deserted me and Dad to be a free spirit or find herself or follow her bliss or whatever. I figured she just got sick of being a dentist's wife in a Philadelphia suburb. First she followed her bliss to California, and then for some reason her bliss took her back to the Milwaukee suburb where *she* grew up. She got a job as a librarian in the public library, which is where she's been ever since.

It wasn't as if she totally abandoned us. All that time, she called every Sunday to tell us how sorry she was and why she'd done what she did. I talked to her a few times, but when she tried to explain, she just kept getting tangled, and nothing she said made sense. After a while, I told my dad to tell her I didn't feel like talking. I didn't want to hear her talk about finding her authentic self.

It was weirdly quiet and sad in the house with just my dad and me, but somehow we got along. Of course, I would have appreciated the peace and quiet more if I'd known how much worse it was going to be when Joan and Josh Darling moved in and supposedly cheered up our sad little family.

I'd been pretty mystified when Dad and Joan started dating, and then when they got married. I thought that Dad had married her just to get even with Mom. I knew he hadn't gotten together with Joan for her chocolate chip cookies.

Even though I was already ten, they made me be the flower girl at the wedding. Joan nagged and pleaded and bullied me into dressing up in a frilly pink princess dress and scattering rose petals from a basket. I flung the petals down the aisle of the church as if they were tennis balls that might bounce. No one noticed. They were too busy admiring Josh Darling, whom Joan dolled up in a pastel blue tuxedo with a ruffled shirt and short pants, and who got to carry the ring on a velvet pillow bigger than his head.

At first I was really upset that Joan was sleeping in my mom's bed, but pretty soon I got used to it, and I could hardly remember when Mom had slept there. Joan was also divorced. I always thought that Dad should have had a man-to-man talk with Joan's ex-husband to find out who Joan really was. One of the things I found hardest about our Brady Bunch combined–family life was how often Dad agreed with Joan, even when she was wrong, and how everything Josh Darling did was perfect, while all I did was make one mistake after another.

In fact, it was as if *I* was the huge mistake that Joan was trying to correct. What I ate, what I wore, how much TV I watched—Joan was full of helpful suggestions that were really criticisms disguised as advice. Maisie, why don't you wear your hair like that pretty girl over there? Maisie, why don't you throw out those smelly sneakers and wear some tight, uncomfortable heels? Maisie, try on this flouncy skirt—it would look so attractive on you. What she really wanted was to change me into a miniature Joan.

As soon as my dad remarried, it drove my mom over the edge, and she started calling every day, sometimes twice a day, theoretically to see how I was adjusting to my new stepfamily. I remember thinking: *If Mom and Dad are still so obsessed with each other, they should have stayed together.* And though you'd imagine that having to deal with Wicked Stepmother Joan would have made me miss and appreciate Mom more, it only made me angrier. It was all Mom's fault. If she'd stayed home and found her bliss in Germantown, or even Philadelphia, none of this would be happening.

Then, two years ago, I picked up the phone, and it was Mom. Before I could tell her that I was so busy that I had to hang up, Mom said, "Good news, darling! Geoff and I have gotten married! And—you don't have to decide right away, take your time and think it over— but now that I'm finally settled, I'm wondering if you want to come live with us. Maybe you could just give it a try—"

I knew she'd had a serious boyfriend for the last year

or so. Dad had let that slip. But now, it seemed, Mom and this guy had a house—guess where? In the blissed-out suburbs of Milwaukee. A big beautiful home they couldn't wait to share with me. Mom's new husband was a math professor at the local community college. I'd always hated math. It was strange, how Geoff's job seemed to make my dad jealous—competitive, maybe—even though everyone knows that dentists make way more money than math professors.

Mom started begging me to come out to Wisconsin and live with her and Geoff. I knew that suburbs were suburbs: Milwaukee, Philadelphia, it would have been the same place. Same malls, same trees, same schools. The same kids, probably. And living with Mom and Geoff would probably be a lot like living with Dad and Joan, only minus annoying Josh Darling. Geoff didn't have any kids of his own—or anyway, none that I knew of. And somehow I had the feeling that Geoff didn't wear hooker underwear, and that he wouldn't be especially interested in turning me into a younger version of himself.

When my mom suggested my coming out to live

with her, it might have seemed like a good idea—if only to get even with Joan and make everybody realize what a bad job Joan was doing of being Sitcom Mom. I think I could have forgiven Mom, that's how much Joan annoyed me.

But to be honest, the main thing that stopped me was: My friends were here. Shakes and Chris and Kevin. I couldn't make friends like that anywhere else. It would be sort of like starting my whole life over from scratch.

I can't remember a time before the four of us were friends. I've known them practically since I was born. To be exact, I've known them since preschool. In fact, our preschool was called Little Friends. And that was what we became.

When we were toddlers, nobody thought it was the tiniest bit strange that my three best friends were boys. And by the time we got to grade school, we'd already been friends for so long that it seemed perfectly normal. I was friends with them before I figured out, from watching the kids around us, that girls were supposed to play with girls, and boys were supposed to hang out with boys. But by then, I wasn't going to drop my best friends and find appropriate new female friends.

Chris and Kevin and Shakes were the kids I had play-dates with on weekends and hung out with after school. They were the first ones I invited to my birthday parties, the ones I wanted to sit next to in class. And from kindergarten on, we were on the same bus route.

First I got on the bus, then Shakes, then Kevin, then Chris. We saved seats for each other, and our seats moved steadily back through the bus until we grabbed the last row. We knew that when we started ninth grade, we would be demoted and exiled all the way to the front of the bus again and have to slowly work our way back until we were seniors. By which point, we'd be able to drive, so it wouldn't matter.

Mostly, on the weekends, we walked to the town park and played games that involved a lot of running around and yelling and pushing each other. I never felt that my friends went easy on me because I was a girl. I was as strong and tough as they were, I ran as fast and yelled as loud. In the summer we swam at the town pool and played basketball. In the winter we watched DVDs, usually in Shakes's basement, and played video games.

No one at school seemed to think I was strange. No one even called me a tomboy.

I just *liked* being around them. It was easy, it was fun. They'd known me before my mom and dad's divorce, so I never had to explain the difficult and personal parts of my life. I never had to give them all the background information that would bring them up to date.

In every bunch of friends, I guess, people get assigned certain roles they play in the group—and then they *become* that person. Kevin was the goofy one who could always make us laugh. Chris was the sweet one who smoothed things over if we got on each other's nerves, which hardly ever happened. And Shakes was . . . well, he was just amazing. I never stopped being impressed that someone with so many physical problems could figure out how to get around his disabilities and hold his own, even if we were playing basketball or video games that required major hand-eye coordination.

I used to love to watch Shakes meet new people. "I'm Shakes," he'd say. You couldn't help but appreciate the fact that a kid with some weird kind of palsy, even a mild case like Shakes's, would make you call him that, and *dare* you to react.

I admired Shakes for being so tough and cool. Even when something was hard for him, he never whined or complained, he never even seemed discouraged. He'd just laugh that funny crooked laugh, and find his own way to do whatever he wanted. There was something really special about him, as if his having been born a little messed up had taught him a different and better way of being a human being. He was always nice to the kids whom the other kids picked on.

Even when he was little, you could see him stopping and thinking before he said anything, maybe because it was harder for him to talk. And he'd say these totally poetic things. Once when we were at Chris's house, watching some honeybees fly around, Shakes said you could watch them singing to each other and thanking the flowers for their nectar. In grade school, he was elected class president more often than anyone else—not because the other kids felt sorry for him, but because even people who hardly knew him could see what a model human being he was.

Unfortunately, his health problems weren't limited

to tics and twitches. Shakes missed school a lot. Not weeks or months or anything, but he spent more time out than most kids. And I knew he spent a lot of that time going to see various doctors and specialists.

But when he came back to school after being away, you weren't supposed to notice that he'd been gone. You didn't ask Shakes how he was. Somehow you knew not to do that. You always took up exactly where you'd left off before he was out sick, as if you were finishing a sentence that had been interrupted in the middle.

Because we weren't allowed to ask him how he was feeling, I got used to looking closely at him, to see how he was. I'd stare at him especially hard when he'd come back from being absent, as if to reassure myself that he was still okay. So maybe the fact that I looked at him longer and more carefully than I looked at the others was also why I felt I knew him better than I knew Chris and Kevin. And I knew them really well.

Sometimes I wondered if Shakes had developed other abilities—extrasensory powers—to make up for his physical troubles. We all thought he was psychic. He often called or emailed or text-messaged me at the exact moment I was thinking about calling or emailing or text-messaging him. And lots of times I'd think of some song, and Shakes would start to hum it. Kevin and Chris and I joked that we'd better not have any negative thoughts about Shakes, because he would know. Actually, we never thought anything negative about Shakes, so it was never a problem.

And what about me? Who was I in the group? Before my mom and dad split up, I was just another kid. But after that, I was the angry one—which translated into the nervy one, the daredevil, the one who acted first and thought about it later.

On Halloween, I was the one who went up to the scary house on our street and rang the doorbell. I was the one who climbed the fence and got our ball when someone hit it into the yard whose owners had the snarly dog. And when a teacher announced that anyone who said one more word would get detention, I was the one who said that fatal one more word. Maybe it would have seemed strange to someone else—someone who wasn't one of us—that I, the girl, was the one who took all the biggest dares and ran the biggest risks. But we didn't think like that, we didn't think about being a boy or a girl. At least not yet, not then.

I used to have friends who were fun to hang out with. Friends I cared about, and who cared about me. And now I've lost that. I've lost all of that. It's true that some bad stuff happened, but maybe we could have forgotten it if not for the TV show inside Joan's head, the lawyer-courtroom drama in which she gets to play the brave, heroic stepmom of the girl who's been assaulted—no, *molested*, no, *inappropriately touched*—by her three best friends.

I'm still thinking about the dream, and about Doctor Atwood asking me what it means—isn't the answer obvious?—as Joan slides the tray of chocolate chip cookies into the oven. Under her apron she's wearing a skirt that's way shorter than what I would wear if I were a mother and a professional psychotherapist Joan's age.

Because if we're talking about *inappropriate*, what about the way Joan dresses! And what about her wanting me to dress like that, too! Joan keeps trying to do all sorts of mother-daughter bonding stuff, like shopping trips to the mall. It always creeps me out, because Joan insists on trying on—and buying—outfits you'd expect to see on some slutty high school girl. She always seems disappointed when I buy jeans and sneakers and T-shirts. That's when she really shows how mean she can be. She'll pick up some filmy little Band-Aid of a dress and say, "This would look so pretty on you, Maisie, if you just lost a little weight." It's evil, pure evil. I'm not even fat. I just have big boobs.

Everything Joan does is embarrassing. She has a boxing coach who makes her run up and down the steps of city hall, like Rocky Balboa, at nine o'clock in the morning, when the whole town can see!

Now, Joan turns away from the oven, straightens up, and when she faces me, she actually claps her hands with joy.

"Cookies in ten minutes, Maisie dear! Chocolate chip!"

"Thanks, I'm not hungry," I say.

CHAPTER FOUR

It's strange how sometimes you can turn your back for one minute—one minute—and by the time you turn around, the whole world's completely different. My mom—my real mom—says that about computers, and cell phones, and the most basic technical stuff. My dad is always blathering on, if you let him, about how drastically dentistry has changed since he started out in the profession.

Of course, when I finally left Dad and Josh Darling

and the Evil Stepmother and went to live with Mom and Geoff, I stayed away a lot longer than a minute. I stuck it out for a whole school year. Eighth grade, as it happened. Unfortunately, for me. It's hard to believe that it was only last year. It seems like another lifetime.

Why did I imagine that life with Mom and Geoff would be any better than life with Dad and Joan? I guess I wasn't thinking all that clearly. I was fighting with Joan all the time. She was getting nastier, letting her true nature show. Every so often, I'd complain to Dad, but he only shrugged and looked sad and said that it was a pity that Joan and I didn't get along better and appreciate each other's good points. Which made me think that Joan was probably complaining about me, too.

I'd only met Geoff once, when he and Mom came to Philadelphia for some sort of academic conference. I think he was interviewing for a better job, which he didn't get. Geoff seemed mind-blowingly dull—but nice enough. Harmless, you might say. I began to think that living with him might be an improvement over Sitcom Mom Joan, who was anything but harmless.

Sitcom Mom insisted we eat dinner "as a family"

every night. She was constantly telling us about these horribly dysfunctional households she was seeing in her practice—imagine, they actually ate their evening meal in front of the TV! No wonder the American family was in so much trouble! She liked to quote statistics and studies that proved that the combination of food and television led to poor grades, juvenile delinquency, drug abuse, obesity—and worse. Joan loved saying "and worse" in a scary, tragic tone, but, knowing Joan, I couldn't imagine what she thought was worse than obesity.

At those moments I tried not to look at my dad, who was trying not to look at me, so neither of us would have to acknowledge that that was what we used to do when we lived with Mom. We often ate with the TV on. We'd liked it, it had felt comfortable. And it didn't mean we never talked, or that we weren't close. We had our conversations at other times—breakfast and bedtime, for example. But maybe Joan was right about the TV not helping families stay together. It certainly hadn't done much for our family.

Those long-ago dinners with Mom and the TV seem like heaven now compared to the torture meals with Joan making me and Josh finish our sentences and keep our elbows off the table. Elbows off the table! Is my dad hearing *that*? And why doesn't he defend me as I plunk my elbows down beside my plate and keep them there until Joan flips out and starts asking why I'm trying to undermine her? Undermine *her*? It has nothing to do with her. Okay, *almost* nothing. Elbows off the table isn't who we *are*. But that isn't quite true, either. It isn't who we used to be. We *are* those no-elbows people now. And I don't recognize us.

Anyway, it's only *my* elbows that have to be off the table. Darling Josh can put his entire face in the plate, and Joan will say, Josh, darling, look at how much you're enjoying your food!

So I was also getting a little sick of Josh doing everything right and me doing everything wrong and my dad not sticking up for me.

Every evening, there was an argument. Dinner became such a nightmare that, if I were Joan, I would have welcomed the noise and distraction of TV. Things got so tense that Darling Josh stopped eating, and *then*, let me tell you, everyone got worried. I felt a little guilty.

Honestly, I had nothing against Darling Josh. The poor kid had had to live with Joan since—well, even before—he was born.

I couldn't help thinking that they wouldn't notice if *I* never ate. They wouldn't notice if I choked and fell off my chair and turned blue. It made me want to be even more unpleasant to Joan, so another fight would start. She'd ask me a simple question—How was school? Did I like my teachers?—and I'd say, "Why do you care? I don't know why you're asking since you don't really care."

So I can't pretend that every argument was Joan's fault. But she couldn't let anything go. She'd whine on and on about how she was trying to be loving and caring, and I was heartless and ungrateful and had no reason to treat her that way. Which I didn't, I guess.

Anyway, I kept thinking that she was only pretending to be hurt. I had the feeling that everything she said was something she'd learned in therapy school or that she'd scripted, in her mind, for her imaginary TV show. If she was as anti-television as she claimed, why did she act—and dress!—like a character on a soap opera?

All this time, Mom was still calling, asking me to live with her. And so one night, after a particularly wicked Joan-fight, I said yes. Okay, fine. I'll come out at the start of the school year.

I guess I wasn't really thinking about the consequences of my decision. To tell the truth, I wasn't thinking at all. I was just so angry at Joan.

Dad pretended to be against my going to Wisconsin, but I think he was secretly relieved, and he agreed that "a little cooling-off time"—I knew he'd gotten the expression from Joan—might make family life go more smoothly when I came back. He didn't seem to think that the move was permanent. So maybe he knew more about Mom and Geoff than I did.

Only Kevin and Chris and Shakes were sad. They were so destroyed, they actually *told* me they were sad, even though it was completely uncool for boys to say how sad they were.

I knew they were the only ones who would really miss me. They warned me not to go. But they also knew how obnoxious Joan was. They were the ones I called and emailed and texted after family fights when I was supposedly "cooling off" in my room.

I think they kind of respected me for finding a way—a pretty extreme way—to let Joan know what a monster I thought she was. They thought I was brave and cool to move halfway across the country just to show the world that I preferred my real mother to the Wicked Stepmom.

Eventually, Kevin and Chris got used to the idea of my leaving. Shakes was the only one who kept telling me not to go. It was August, and I was about to leave so that I could start the school year in Wisconsin. He and I were sitting on big boulders right in the middle of a stream that ran through the state park, which we could bike to. The sunlight dappled the rocks and danced across the water. I'd had to give Shakes a helping hand as we walked from stone to stone. I was afraid he'd miss a step and fall into the stream, but he never did. He made it seem like an adventure. Like we were explorers, Lewis and Clark. Or Peter Pan and Wendy.

I remember Shakes saying, "You're shooting your-self in the foot, dude. Trust me. It's going to be worse there than it is here." I don't know how he knew. Maybe it was that special intuition, that ESP of his. Maybe he meant that it would be harder for me without him and the other guys around. I remember every word he said that day. I especially remember him calling me *dude*. Because after I got back, a year later, none of them ever called me *dude* again.

I remember telling Shakes, "If I'm going to shoot myself in some body part, better the foot than the head."

But I might as well have aimed for my head, and gotten it over with. Because living with Mom and Geoff was pretty much like going slowly brain-dead.

In the beginning, Geoff was just dull. I'd never met a human being who could talk about himself so much and have so little to say. By the time I'd been there two weeks, I was the world's number-one expert on Geoff. Not counting Mom, I suppose.

I knew where he'd grown up (Detroit), the games he'd played as a kid, every course he'd taken in middle school, every teacher he'd had during his fabulous college career at Wayne State. Then the years of graduate school, and the PhD thesis that some big deal professor had said showed some original promise. Some original promise? That was Geoff's moment of glory, Geoff's fifteen minutes of fame. It had all been downhill since then.

And now? Now Geoff did nothing but complain about how hard he worked, how little he got paid, and how retarded his students were. I felt sorry for his students, who probably didn't know he said they were idiots who couldn't add two and two. But to hear Geoff tell it, they worshipped the ground he walked on.

Geoff wasn't even good looking. He was tall and beaky and bald, with a shiny, bullet-shaped dome head. Believe me, he wasn't the type of guy who'd be anybody's favorite teacher. He wore those corny professor jackets with leather patches on the elbows. I wondered where Geoff shopped. Thrift shops, I imagined. Geoff was cheap. God forbid an avocado cost ten cents more than it did last week. Geoff could spend a whole meal on the subject of one overpriced avocado.

Whenever Geoff went on about himself and how much everything cost, Mom would nod and smile as if everything Geoff was saying was fascinating and new, though probably she'd heard it a million times before I even got there. I guess Mom didn't know Geoff well enough, or feel comfortable enough, to suggest we have dinner in front of the TV. She seemed to really believe that Geoff was smarter and more interesting than she was. I could see where she'd got that idea. It was definitely what Geoff thought. But I could have told her that he wasn't half as intelligent as she was. I mean half as intelligent as she used to be.

It occurred to me that, from a kid's point of view, having your parents remarry was sort of like watching them get brainwashed. Something—someone—forced them, little by little, day by day, to think and say things that they would never have thought or said before.

Secretly, I kept hoping that the brainwashing would wear off, and that the new marriages would self-destruct. I knew that every kid from a divorced family fantasizes about her parents getting back together. Still, I couldn't help it. My other fantasy was that Joan and Geoff would meet and realize that *they* were made for each other. I imagined them running off together and leaving Mom and Dad to console each other, and maybe fall back in love, after they'd bonded over the subject of what creeps they'd married.

Anyway, life with Mom and Geoff deteriorated rapidly. After a few weeks, Geoff must have decided that I was so impressed by Important Mathematical Genius Geoff that he could relax and let Spoiled Brat Geoff come out.

CHAPTER FIVE

Mom had cooked chicken pot pie, which was one of my favorite dishes. I scarfed mine down as soon as I was served. By the time I looked up, Geoff was prodding his food with his fork and looking as if he'd found a dead rat baked inside the flaky crust.

"Jeanette, do you know how salty this is? Have you tasted it? Are you trying to kill me? Are you trying to send my blood pressure skyrocketing through the roof?"

He threw his bowl like a discus, skimming it across the tabletop. It clattered to the floor. I watched flecks of chicken and potato and cream hit the walls, like blood splatter in a horror film. Then Geoff stalked out of the room.

"I guess his blood pressure's *already* through the roof," I said.

"Oh, dear," was all my mother said.

"Excuse *me*?" I said to Mom. "I thought it was delicious."

But Mom only shrugged and got a sponge and started cleaning the walls and the floor.

After that, Geoff's tantrums got worse. He was never violent or threatening. Nor was his fury always directed at us, exactly. Once, when he couldn't find a piece of paper he needed to do his income taxes, he hit himself in the head so hard that the college honor society ring he always wore broke the skin and blood trickled down his forehead.

Once, when his tie came back from the cleaners with a stain still on it, he got a pair of scissors and cut out the dirty spot and told my mom to take it back to the cleaners so they would know what he was talking about. Once, for some reason I can't remember, he had to pick me up from school. A teacher had kept us a few minutes late, and when I finally ran out the door and got into Geoff's car, he screeched away from the curb so fast that the whole school turned to look.

At moments like that, I was glad that no one in the school knew me. Otherwise, it might have bothered me that I hadn't made one single friend. Nobody was mean to me, nor did they try to make me feel like a freak or an outsider. They just didn't seem all that interested in me, in where I'd come from, or who I was. They all seemed to feel as if getting to know me would be too much work. They'd all known each other practically since birth. They had all the friends they needed already, so why should they bother making a new one? Or maybe they sensed something I didn't know myself. I wasn't going to stick around all that long, so why should they go to the trouble?

Also, I kept thinking that because I'd become friends with Kevin and Chris and Shakes so early and stayed friends with them for so long, I'd never learned—I'd never had to learn—how to actually *make* friends. It was as if I'd missed school on the day they taught that lesson. Maybe there was some trick to it, something you could do to make other kids want to hang out with you. I didn't get it, and I *totally* didn't get how to make friends with other girls—which, I knew, was what I should have been doing. Half the time, I didn't understand what the girls in my new school were talking about, or why they cared about the things—clothes and makeup and movie-star gossip—that seemed important to them. I didn't know how to start a conversation with them, and after a while I stopped trying. I knew my mom was sort of worried about it, but she had enough to deal with, coping with Geoff's temper tantrums.

I could handle the loneliness. But the bad news was, I had no one to tell about what a baby Geoff was. I emailed and texted Shakes and Kevin and Chris. But it wasn't the same as being in the same town and seeing them every day. Sometimes it took them—even Shakes—a few days to answer, by which point I'd forgotten which one of Geoff's fits I'd been complaining about. At least Geoff had no interest in acting like a father. He never said,

"Call me Dad." I don't think he had any desire for me to think of him as my dad. *He* was the baby that Mom had signed on to take care of. Which made *me* the ugly stepsister, the rival for Mom's affections.

Geoff's impersonation of a grown-up reminded me of Joan's Brady Bunch Mom act, her *Doctor Joan Marbury, Therapist* miniseries. The difference was that Geoff occasionally stopped acting and let his true self creep out. So that was another thing that Mom and Dad had in common. Both of them seemed to have a weakness for bad actors.

Meanwhile, Dad and Joan seemed to have some kind of weird intuition for when Geoff had just had a major tantrum. That's usually when the phone would ring, and it would be Dad or Joan, or both of them on separate extensions, calling to see how I was doing.

"Fine," I'd say.

Then Joan would say she heard something in my voice that she didn't like. If my dad wasn't already on the phone, she'd put him on. He was supposed to tell me: If I wanted to come back and stay with them, I had only to say the word.

The *word*? What she really meant was *words*. I knew

which words Joan wanted to hear. *Joan, I mean Mom, I've finally come to my senses and realized you're a better mother than my real mom ever was.* Joan was competing with my mother just like Dad was competing with Geoff. I couldn't help wondering: What were they competing *for*?

Another thing I wondered was: What if I'd "said the word" right before Christmas, when they and Josh Darling went to the Bahamas for the holidays, and never told me, let alone asked if I wanted to come along? What word, exactly, would I have said. *Help*? Would that have done it? I guess I must not have said the right word, because I didn't go back to Pennsylvania even once during that whole school year I lived in Wisconsin. Dad and Joan always had something important to do during my school vacations.

One night, after dinner, Mom had gone to a board meeting at the library, where she worked. I was watching *Top Chef*.

Geoff came home from teaching. He walked into the living room and sat down in the chair. He kept shooting me filthy looks because I guessed he thought I was supposed to jump up and offer him the couch. And I probably should have, but I didn't want to.

Geoff said, "Hand me the remote, will you, Maisie?" I very politely asked Geoff if he'd mind waiting until the end of the show, so I could see who won. I wasn't trying to be difficult. I'd learned my lesson from being around Joan. I'd never get satisfaction.

Geoff said, "Actually, I *do* mind." Then he did a surprising thing, by which I mean a thing that surprised even me, and by then I was so used to Geoff, I was rarely surprised by the childish stuff he did.

Geoff stood up and came over to me and grabbed the remote from my hand. I was so shocked, I held on to it, so that for while we were sort of wrestling for the remote, like kids. Except that Geoff wasn't a kid. He was stronger. He got it. He won.

I stood up and watched him victoriously—triumphantly!—switch from channel to channel. Click click. Are you getting this, Maisie?

He said, very fake-calm, as if we hadn't just practically had a physical fight, "We pay a fortune for a hundred channels of cable, and there's nothing to watch. We should probably cancel."

When Mom came home, I followed her to her room and told her that I wanted to move back and live with

Dad. I was careful to say *Dad* and not *Dad and Joan*. The school year was just ending, so it was pretty convenient. Mom cried, and made a big show of being sad and hurt, and I guess she really was. But in the end, she did the same thing that Dad did. They both seemed relieved that I was giving them a break in which to try and make their repulsive, brainwashed second marriages work out.

That was how I moved back home in June, as soon as school in Wisconsin ended. Or maybe I should say: that was when I moved back to Pennsylvania, the place that I *thought* of as home—that is, when I'd been in Wisconsin.

The first thing I did after I said hello to Dad and Joan and Josh Darling was go to my room and call Shakes and arrange for him and me and Kevin and Chris to get together. It made me feel better to be talking to Shakes as I looked around my old room and saw how much Joan had "straightened up." Shakes was so glad to hear from me, it took him a few moments to be able to say my name. I wondered if his physical problems had gotten worse in my absence.

It was already evening, and Joan and Dad were making a big production about how tired they were from the travel and stress of picking me up at the airport. And how much I was supposed to appreciate the glorious reunion dinner and us all being together again.

Shakes and I arranged to meet the next day. He'd call Chris and Kevin. If the weather was good, we'd bike to the park. If not, we would meet at Shakes's house and figure out what to do.

In my mind, I was already there. I was polite and pleasant and kept my elbows off the table. I heard, as if from a great distance, Joan yakking on and on about the success she was having with a woman who'd been binge-ing and purging for years. I could tell myself that Joan talking about some puking woman while she expected us to eat was funny, because, in my mind, I'd already gone to a place where I would see my friends, and things *would* be funny, for real.

I couldn't wait for the next day. I was so happy and eager to see them. The good feeling lasted for one night.

Because the next day was when I found out how different everything was and how quickly people can change.

CHAPTER SIX

I woke up to a chilly, drumming rain. No chance of that group bike ride to the park.

Joan dropped me off at Shakes's house on her way to the office, where she was going to snoop around in the private souls of the poor, miserable losers who paid her to hear them spill out all their secrets.

Of course, this was before everyone decided that it would be good for me to see Doctor Atwood. This was before I *became* one of those people, paying someone who didn't want to listen to what I didn't want to say.

My real mom had been a close friend of Marian, Shakes's mom. My mother had no problem babysitting a kid with a mild disability. Later, Shakes told me that, all during that time, he was having seizures. But he never had them around us, so I never saw them. I guess his mom must have warned my mom, and my mom must have said she could handle it just so long as Marian told her what to do if something happened.

I could hardly imagine what Joan would do if a kid had a seizure. Probably scream and call 911 and flirt with the ambulance guys. Whereas Geoff would just wait and do nothing and then accuse the poor kid of faking a seizure just to divert attention from the person everyone should have been paying attention to—namely, Geoff.

Marian knew she could leave Shakes with Mom. So when we were little, Shakes and I got to hang out even more than we otherwise would have.

The only problem with Marian was that you had to stay on your toes, because you couldn't call Shakes *Shakes* around her. She'd say, "His name is Edward." Otherwise,

I'd always liked her. But I liked her even more when Joan dropped me off at her house, and Marian couldn't have been chillier to her.

Marian said, "Doctor Marbury," and barely opened the front door. I wondered if that was because she was still loyal to Mom, or if Shakes had told her what I'd said about Joan always saying things like, "This dress would look so pretty on you, Maisie, if you shed that extra poundage."

Joan had never tried to make friends with Marian. Shakes's house was my territory. It belonged to him and me, and Chris, and Kevin. Joan had never shadowed it with her evil presence.

Marian pulled me inside the house and shut the door even as Joan was blabbing on about what time she would pick me up. Then Marian squeezed me until I pretend-coughed, and we laughed.

She held me at arm's length and said, "Oh, Maisie! We missed you so much! It feels like you've been gone for a hundred years. My God, look at you. Look how you've grown. You kids are getting so big. Pretty soon, you won't be kids anymore."

I wished she hadn't said that.

"We're really still kids," I said.

"I don't think so, honey." Marian laughed and lightly kissed the top of my head, and my hands flew instinctively to the front of my T-shirt where they covered the breasts I'd grown since the last time I'd been here.

That was another thing —the main thing, really—that had happened in Wisconsin.

I'd gotten a whole new body during my year away. I'd grown breasts and a weird curvy ass. I'd gotten my period, too. I felt like a spectator watching my body do whatever it wanted, without my knowledge or permission. I felt like someone who'd been tricked into thinking she had one body, and now—surprise!—she had another.

I was glad that I was living with my mom when all these changes happened. It was almost as if my body had been thoughtful enough to wait until my real mother was around. Mom was cool. She kept telling me I looked great. She said, "Feel free to ask me anything, Maisie." I knew she meant "anything about sex." But if she couldn't even say *sex*, how could I feel free to ask her about it?

Anyway, there was nothing I wanted to ask. It would have been hell with Joan, listening to her lecture me about the mystery and beauty of being a woman.

Since I didn't have any friends or anyone I could talk to, I spent my time in Wisconsin secretly checking out other girls at school to see if the same thing was happening to them. Which it was—but not as much. They were growing these neat little buds up around their shoulders.

Me, on the other hand . . . I looked in the mirror and turned around, and by the time I turned back, I had these gigantic mega-boobs, the kind movie stars pay fortunes for. I'd gotten them practically overnight, for free. But I didn't want them. Where had they come from, anyway? My mom was small-breasted, so it must have been some rogue gene from a busty great-great-grandmother, lost in the reaches of time.

That was why I'd sort of liked being invisible in my Wisconsin school. I was able to deal with the changes without it being public. No one knew what I'd looked like before, so no one paid attention to how different I looked now.

Marian noticed the moment I walked in her front

door. That was why she looked me up and down and laughed and said I wasn't a kid anymore.

She said, "Maisie, you look lovely. You really do." I don't know why she sounded so sad. Maybe it made her sad to think about us all growing up so fast. Or maybe she saw herself in me. Grown-ups were always doing that.

"I wish your mom were here," she said.

"I was just *at* my mom's, remember? I left."

"I miss her," said Marian.

I said, "Believe me, you'd miss her less if you got to know Geoff."

I was having the weirdest reaction: my own stab of sadness for all the time I'd been away, all the weeks and months I'd missed and that I would never get back. Nearly a whole year without my best friends, a year away from the only kids who cared about me.

Just at that moment, Shakes came up behind his mom.

"Shakes!" I said.

"Edward," Marian said.

"Edward," I said. It always felt strange to call him that, but I suddenly liked how strange it felt. It wasn't weirdly strange. It was familiar strange.

Just as I'd thought when we'd talked on the phone, his twitches, or spasms, or whatever they were, had gotten slightly worse. But maybe I was only paying closer attention because I hadn't seen him in so long. I'd gotten used to the funny movements Shakes couldn't help making, but now I was struck by them all over again. Maybe that was because he looked like a different person—taller, thicker around the middle—a slightly butterball, junior-sized grown-up.

"Shakes?" I said, as if I really had to make sure.

"Edward," Marian said.

"Yo, Maisie." Shakes's voice cracked, and he grinned. "It's . . . it's great to see you." He hadn't gotten much taller, but his face was longer, and he had the faintest dark shadow on his upper lip. It made him seem sort of mysterious, dangerous, and exotic, like a messed-up old-school gangster. His left leg had always dragged slightly, and he did a kind of quick little hitch to propel himself forward. That jerky skip also seemed more pronounced than it had when I'd left.

Back in the day, I would have hugged him. My mom

and Marian both have snapshots of me and Shakes throwing our arms around each other like two babies in a bubble bath commercial. But I didn't hug him now. I raised my arms, and then stopped.

Kevin and Chris were in the basement, watching TV. Kevin had the remote. As I walked downstairs, Chris and Kevin turned and saw me. Their faces lit up, they burst into these gigantic grins—and then Kevin changed the channel.

Just before he did, I saw a flash of two blue dots dancing on the chest of a half-naked blond girl. The guys were watching one of those programs about college kids getting drunk in Mexico or Florida or some other frat-boy vacation hot spot. We used to imitate the dumb beefy guys slurring their speech and yelling the same stupid things over and over.

Chris and Kevin looked at me as if I'd caught them doing something really wicked. As if I were their mom. And then something strange happened in their faces. It was almost as if they were looking at me from the opposite end of a telescope, and I was growing smaller. I felt as if I was being accused of some crime I didn't commit. For some reason, tears popped into my eyes, and I blinked them away.

Chris and Kevin had changed, too. They weren't kids anymore, but they weren't men, either. They weren't even teenage boys. They seemed to have stalled at some bizarre in-between stage. They'd both gotten sort of plump—girlish, in a way. They reminded me of turtles separated from their shells. They looked as if they would squeal if I poked them.

I'd noticed something similar happening with the boys I'd gone to school with in Wisconsin. A lot of them went through a homely phase and got sort of soft and round, with those funny, cracking voices. They got these huge Adam's apples that always made me think of babies whose teeth are too big for their mouths. Then suddenly—it often seemed like over-night—they'd shoot up and get taller, more muscular. Their voices were strange and deep. But somehow I never imagined it happening to the friends I'd left at home. I thought they'd always be little boys and, no matter how much I changed, they'd look exactly the same as they had on the day I'd left.

"Maisie," said Chris. "You look really good." Chris was always the nice one. Kevin looked at me and squinted, and said, "Holy shit, you grew up." Chris nodded like a maniac.

I knew they were talking about my breasts, though they would never have admitted that. It was almost as if they didn't recognize me, as if they'd never met me. Oh, I should never have gone away! I wouldn't have, if I'd known that I could never come back and have things be the same as they were when I left.

I wanted to wave my arms and say, *Hey, look, it's me, Maisie. We rubbed paste in each other's hair in preschool. Remember me? I'm the same person.*

But I wasn't the same person. For one thing, I had breasts. And if I'd waved my arms, it would only have made my chest stick out more.

For the first time in my life, I almost wished that my best friends had been girls. Then the same things would be happening to us all. Breasts, hips, getting our period—it would bring us closer together instead of forcing us apart.

"How are you?" said Kevin. His voice was different,

too. Not only because three words were enough to make it break up like a weak phone signal, but because of his tone. He sounded stiff and sort of phony, as if he were talking to a *girl*.

"Fine," I said.

"You *look* good," said Chris.

"You already said that, doofus," said Kevin.

Why were they talking about how I *looked*? They'd never done that before. No one thought about how anyone looked. We had just looked like ourselves. I wished they would relax so that we could just *be* ourselves.

"Leave her alone," said Shakes, reading my mind. At least he could still do that. "She's fine. She's . . . Maisie."

"How was living with your mom?" asked Chris. "Not that great, I guess, if you're back here. So how come you came home?"

It made me happy that they called it *home*. But I couldn't figure out why they didn't know why I'd left Wisconsin. They knew everything about me. It took me a few minutes to remember that I'd stopped emailing and calling them months ago, probably because they'd stopped emailing and calling me.

"Mom was cool," I said. "But the guy she married makes Joan look like a cross between Mother Theresa and Albert Einstein."

"Wow," said Shakes. "How could your mom and dad both have made such messed-up choices?"

"Good question," I said. "I asked myself that a hundred times a day. Geoff is a total freak."

They were giving me strange looks, and I wondered if they were thinking that maybe I'd been molested or something. That was the story you heard every time you turned on the TV. I read a novel for kids about that: My pervert stepdad groped me. He threatened to kill me if I told.

"Not *that* kind of freak," I said. "He didn't hit on me or beat me or sneak into my room at night or anything like that. He was just like this . . . spoiled brat." I couldn't explain it. They would have had to have been there every time Geoff acted like a two-year-old.

"It's good you came back," said Shakes, and then they all fell silent.

"A lot happened since you went away," Chris said.

"Like what?"

"Like nothing," Kevin said. "I guess you must have forgotten that nothing ever happens in this town. Somebody's cat got run over. When was that?"

"I don't remember," Chris said. "But it was totally sad."

"Come on," I said. "What did I miss?"

All three of them started giggling. I looked from one to the other. We never used to have private jokes that left one person out.

"Chris has a girlfriend," said Kevin.

"She's *not* my girlfriend," said Chris.

"She is, actually," said Kevin. "Your girlfriend."

"Who is she?" I said.

"It's Daria," Shakes said. And he made a face, though maybe I just thought that, because with Shakes you sometimes can't tell a face from a twitch.

"Daria Wells?" I said. "You're kidding." Daria was the world's nerdiest math genius. Kids teased her, they called her Pocket Protector Girl. But they didn't tease her that much, because she was so smart. Everyone used to say she was going to grow up to become the world's richest investment banker.

"No, you should see her," Chris said. "She's, like, really pretty now."

"Are you guys trying to tell me that Daria Wells is a *hottie*?"

Chris turned literally purple. "What's on TV?" he said.

"See that?" said Kevin. "She *is* his girlfriend. Better be careful what you say."

I felt suddenly tired from the effort of trying to figure out how exactly Daria would fit into our gang, the three of them and me. Meanwhile, they kept trying to look at my face, but their own faces were frozen from the strain of not checking out my breasts. I told myself, They'll get used to the new me. That'll just be who I am now. Maisie, their best friend from preschool. Only now their old pal has breasts.

"Chris and Daria are having sex," said Kevin.

"No way," said Chris. "It depends what you mean by sex."

"You ask Daria that?" said Kevin.

Once more, Chris and Kevin giggled and snorted through their noses. Who *were* these dorky guys? The funny thing was, Shakes kept looking back and forth between me and the two guys, as if he was trying to figure out how he should be acting. Or maybe he'd just developed some new twitch when I was gone.

Kevin said, "Everyone saw them kissing in the hall outside the girls' bathroom."

Chris said, "Kissing isn't sex." And they laughed again. I wasn't getting the joke.

After a silence, I said, "So what *is* on TV?"

"Let's find out," said Shakes.

They took the sofa. I grabbed a chair, and Kevin hit the remote.

"*Pimp My Ride*. Cool," I said.

They all seemed a little surprised, but pleased, as if they'd been thinking that a person with breasts would insist on watching some girl show like *My Super Sweet Sixteen*. Slowly, the pressure leaked out of the room, like air from a punctured bike tire, as we watched the transformation of a wannabe Hollywood actor's ten-year-old, beat-up Lincoln Town Car into a movie star limo with a screening room built in behind the backseat.

"Pathetic!" said Kevin.

"Loser!" I said. I could feel them relax a little more. Breasts or no breasts, I was still Maisie, who could still insult the people who got makeovers on TV. Next we watched a segment about a girl who worked for a veterinarian, picking up ill pets and returning them cured, getting her mom's station wagon all cheesed up and made over into a vehicle with a comfy dog bed that folded down into a dog run. I wished the girl hadn't squealed in such a high-pitched soprano. I felt as if my friends were blaming me for how girly and ridiculous she sounded.

I said, "So what have you guys been doing besides kissing girls and watching TV?"

Shakes said, "Making movies. I got a camera for my birthday."

"What kind of movies?"

"Short films. Stupid stuff," Shakes said. "But we put one up on YouTube and got more than a thousand hits."

"What was it about?" I asked.

"I play Shakes the Detective," he said. "These guys take turns being the murderer and the murder victim."

I said, "If there were four of us, you could have a

crime-solving partner."

"Or the victim could be a girl," Kevin said.

"I guess it could," I agreed. No one spoke for a while.

I said, "I could pretend to fall off a roof. You could film me going out a window, and then cut to a shot of me lying facedown on the ground."

"That would be cool," Shakes said. "But you wouldn't always have to be the one who gets killed."

"Yeah," I said. "That would be good."

All of a sudden, it was like I was back in the club, though no one could have said what I'd done, or what it had taken, to be readmitted. They were glad to have me back, and I was glad to be there.

CHAPTER SEVEN

We got through the rest of the summer. We had fun. It was just like before. Though actually, it wasn't, not exactly. It was *sort of* just like before.

Now, when the guys went swimming, I pretended I had something else to do. If they saw me in my bathing suit, it might undo all the hard work I was doing to make them see me as the same person I was before I'd left. Or anyway, the same person in an older person's body.

We made two episodes in the *Shakes the Detective* series. They were smart and funny and amazingly good considering we made them for no money with Shakes's handheld camera. The best part was thinking them up. All of us had ideas, and we'd shout them out; it didn't seem to matter which person had the idea.

Even though Shakes had said I didn't always have to be the murder victim, that's how it worked out. I told myself I didn't care. I was the only girl. Since we seemed to have started thinking that way—who was a girl and who was a boy—I figured I might as well take advantage of everything that made me a girl. That is, besides having big boobs. It always seemed more criminal and tragic if the victim was a girl and more satisfying when Shakes found out whether Kevin or Chris was the perp. The films were sort of a cross between mystery and science fiction. As soon as Shakes figured out who'd done the deed, I—the victim—would immediately come back from the dead. And later, at home, Shakes would score the film to a woozy, outer-space sound track.

Once, we were shooting in the town park, and Daria Wells walked by. She didn't seem at all surprised to see us, so I figured that she and Chris had talked, and he'd told her we would be there. I couldn't see how the boys thought she'd gotten so hot. She still looked chunky and snooty. Her breasts weren't nearly as big as mine. It struck me how weird it was even to be thinking like that. But as I looked at her, I sort of got why Chris liked her. Either she'd gotten taller, or she held herself tall. She no longer rounded her shoulders. She looked really comfortable with the whole *thing* of being a girl. It seemed strange that she could get away with it, being as smart as she was. Obviously, math wasn't the only thing she was smart at.

In a high, unnatural voice, Chris said, "Hey, Daria! Want to be in our movie? We could write you in."

We could? I thought.

"Oh, no, thank you, Chris," Daria said. "Acting isn't my thing. I'd prefer to produce someday."

Produce? I thought. *Pathetic!*

"Gosh," said Chris. "That's amazing. I'll bet you'd really be good at it."

Shakes and I looked at each other and rolled our eyes. It was hard not to laugh. Only then did I realize that I'd been a little worried ever since Chris asked her to be in our movie.

Actually, acting was Daria's thing. She made a big show of being superior and bored.

Finally, she said, "Bye, I guess."

I said, "Bye, she *guesses*?" Shakes started to laugh, or maybe he was just shaking. Then I saw him look at Chris, and turn away and do his funny, hop-walk a few steps away, and then back.

In fact, our film wasn't boring at all, though maybe that episode might have been better if Daria hadn't made everybody self-conscious.

That was the episode in which Kevin shot and then strangled me because I'd cheated on him with Chris. In the installment after that, my body washed up on the shore of the lake and the three of them had to figure out who had killed me, and why. I can't remember the details. I could look it up on YouTube. I could watch how happy we were that summer before school started. Or how happy we were *trying* to be. But it was happy, really, compared to what came after.

That's why I don't want to watch it, though I think

about it when I'm on YouTube. I know better than to go there. It would break my heart to see us still being best friends before we reached the point of no return, the point where we are now—the point at which I'm the accuser, and my best friends are the defendants. This time, Shakes the Detective can't solve the crime and make everything all right.

CHAPTER EIGHT

Doctor Atwood says, "There's one part of the story I don't understand."

"*One* part?" I say. "You don't understand *one part*? There's a zillion and one parts of the story I don't get. So maybe if you tell me what that one part is, I can ask you about the other zillion."

"I'm sorry," says Doctor Atwood. "Obviously, there are mysteries here that need to be cleared up. That's why you're coming to see me, Maisie. So we can figure it out together. Maybe I should have said there's one *detail* that I don't get."

"Try me," I say. I make my eyes go out of focus, and I concentrate on one of Doctor Atwood's masks, until its eyes swim together and it turns into Cyclops. I can tell she thinks she's onto something big. Maybe she imagines that she's going to catch me in one of those tiny slipups that give the whole case away when the cops are interviewing a suspect on TV. Something that will prove I'm lying, that the *incident* didn't happen the way I say it did.

Isn't that what this is all about? Someone has to be lying. Either it's me, or it's Chris and Kevin and Shakes. Are these sessions with Doctor Atwood all about finding out whether the liar is me? I tell myself I'm just being a paranoid teen. Joan believes me, and she was the one who suggested I go see Doctor Atwood. The reason she set this up isn't because she thinks I'm lying when I say the guys touched my breasts even though I told them not to. Or maybe it's a legal thing, maybe they'll call Doctor Atwood as their expert witness.

The problem is, it's all gotten pretty jumbled. There's the story I first told Joan, the story that got repeated, the story I told after that, the story I'm telling now. So if Doctor Atwood can help me figure it out, it's worth all the money Dad and Joan are paying.

"Maisie," Doctor Atwood is saying. "Try to focus, all right?"

"Sorry," I say. "What were we talking about?"

Doctor Atwood says, "That one detail. Which is . . . you and your friends are in the ninth grade, right?"

"Right." Hasn't she heard a word I've said?

"And you rode on the high school bus? Which is where it happened?"

"Right again," I say.

"In the backseat?"

"That's correct."

"So here's the part I don't understand. Unless things have changed dramatically since I was a kid, ninth graders don't get to sit in the backseat of the bus. That's senior territory. Reserved for seniors who don't drive yet, or who don't have cars or know anyone with a car. Or the ones who had their license revoked."

I smile. It's the first completely smart thing that Doctor Atwood has ever said.

"Good point."

"So how come you were sitting there, you and your ninth-grade friends?"

I'm glad she asked. Because the answer involves the only part of this whole thing that I still like thinking about. Even though it's going to hurt, I like remembering the way Shakes could be.

I say, "I was the first one on the bus. Just me and the driver, Big Maureen. I'd known that was going to happen. Joan had looked up the bus route, they had it at the post office, and she totally spazzed out that I had the longest ride of any kid in the district. But there was nothing she could do, the school blamed the bus company and vice versa, on and on.

"So I shouldn't have been surprised. But the first day of school, when I got on the bus and realized that I was actually first, I said good morning to Big Maureen and sort of panicked and headed straight to the back of bus. You'd think if I was feeling nervous, I'd have stayed near Big Maureen, but Big Maureen isn't the kind of person you want to stay near. She was never mean or scary, just slumpy and depressed. Joan had told me she was a single mom with five kids who needed the job. It felt weird, to be one of two people on that huge bus. I don't know why. It was almost like Big Maureen and I were in this huge yellow spaceship and we'd blasted off before the rest of the crew had shown up. I was glad when we slowed down to pick up someone else. And I was practically *ecstatic* when I saw we were picking up Shakes. I watched him do his little crablike hop down his driveway. I was so glad to see him, I wished I could have hugged him."

"Why couldn't you?" asks Doctor Atwood.

I say, "Is that a serious question?"

Now it's Doctor Atwood's turn to smile.

"Go on, Maisie," she says.

"It would have been . . . uncomfortable."

Why *couldn't* I have hugged him? Maybe because it would have reminded everybody—that is, Shakes and me—of the fact that now I had a pair of breasts.

I say, "When Shakes got on, I was doing these giant semaphores, waving at him from the back. He smiled this cool loopy grin and he came back and sat next to me.

"Soon after, we crossed the reservoir. We had maybe ten minutes with just the two of us alone on the bus before anyone else got on. The scenery was really pretty there, but it was so early. We were both really tired, and we sort of fell asleep."

Leaning on each other's shoulders.

That's a little *detail* that might help the doctor make sense of all this, but I don't want to tell it. In fact, the more I think about the story—the beginning of the story—the less I want to tell it. I just want to be quiet and think about it, by myself.

I say, "By the time we woke up, two seniors were standing over us. Big lacrosse-team types."

Doctor Atwood laughs, though it's not funny.

Here's what I don't say:

The seniors were both beefy, but one had a sort of sheeplike, lamb-y thing going, too. Mr. Beef and Mr. Lamb was how I thought of them right away.

They told Shakes and me that we were sitting in their seats.

Lamb said, "What part of 'lowly ninth-grade turd' are you midgets not getting?"

"Wow," I said. "I'm amazed that a guy like you

knows a fancy word like *turd*."

They both turned and looked at me, as if they were trying to decide whether or not to do anything about me.

Beef said, "Hey, listen to Little Miss D Cup."

Shakes stood. I pushed him back in his seat. I was so proud and happy that he would stand up for me against these two morons. On the other hand, I didn't want to watch him get trashed.

"How much clearer can we say it? These seats are reserved," said Beef. "We're seniors."

"How come you're not driving?" Shakes asked.

Everything kind of hung in suspension until the seniors looked at each other and laughed.

"Party this summer," Lamb said.

"Freaking blowout," said Beef.

Lamb said, "At the end of the day, some license suspension went down."

"At the end of the *night*, dude." Beef guffawed like a moron.

"Sorry to hear it," Shakes said.

"Thanks," said Lamb. "We appreciate that. You and your girlfriend got to move up front now."

"I'm not his girlfriend," I said. They ignored me.

They actually weren't interested one way or the other.

"I'd like to, I'd really like to," said Shakes. "But I have a disability. It's state-mandated that I sit near the exit"—he nodded at the door between the two back-seats—"or else the county has to pay for one of those buses that stop and kneel down so I can get on. Adds at least another half hour to the ride, especially when we get rerouted so we pick up every crippled kid in the county. Have you ever been on one of those special buses when they have to load on a wheelchair?"

Beef and Lamb groaned. They were too stupid to figure out that by the time buses like that went into service, they would have graduated long before. It wasn't going to happen, anyway. The school board was too cheap.

"What kind of disability do you have?" asked Lamb.

"Watch," said Shakes. The bus was moving faster. Shakes stood up and started down the aisle. One of his legs was wobbly, and he kind of unhinged it further. The bus rounded a curve, and Shakes went into free fall, flying all over the bus, nearly falling. It was a real performance, it was like watching ballet. Or a car chase. At the very last minute, his arm shot out and grabbed the back of a seat.

"Please take your seats, gentlemen," Big Maureen

yelled into her rearview mirror.

"Watch it!" said Beef, who hadn't breathed the whole time Shakes was flopping around in the aisle.

"Hey, man, be careful," said Lamb. "That's dangerous. You wouldn't want to hurt yourself."

"Get your crazy ass in the seat." Beef indicated the backseat.

"Take it easy," Lamb told Shakes. "If I were you, I'd just sit tight until we come to a full stop."

Neither of them wanted to sit next to Shakes. So they let me stay where I was. Beef claimed the seat in front of us, Lamb across the aisle from us, and they sprawled all over the seats so each one had a seat to himself and no one would dream of sitting beside them.

They ignored us; they never talked to us again. From that day on, Shakes and I had the backseat all to ourselves until Beef and Lamb got on. And then the best part of my day was over.

That first day, when Kevin got on, we watched him looking all around the bus for us. Before, we'd always saved seats for him and Chris, and all four of us always sat together. So he was looking for us to figure out where to sit. He looked shocked when he finally saw us in back, with Beef and Lamb like big hunky walls between us and the rest of the bus. Kevin knew better than to try and get past them and invade sacred senior territory so he could sit near me and Shakes. He shrugged and took a seat near the front. He kept turning around and giving us weird, unfriendly looks. Like, what was up with the two of us? Who did we think we were, and why had we deserted them? It was too late for Shakes and me to move up—Big Maureen would have had a fit—and Shakes had already demonstrated what could happen when he tried to walk around when the bus was in motion. Besides, the truth was, I liked sitting next to Shakes in the back. I didn't want to move.

When Chris got in, I watched him when he spotted Kevin—and then Shakes and me. What was going on? He sat beside Kevin, and they talked for a while, and then they both kept turning around and shooting us dirty looks. How come *we* got special treatment? I told myself that Chris didn't mind all that much because Daria Wells was sitting in the seat right in front of his. But in my heart, I knew that something had happened that was more serious than the four of us not sitting together on the bus, and sometimes I think that all our troubles began on that first bus ride.

That's what happened. But this is what I tell Doctor Atwood:

"I don't know why we got to sit in the back. I think it had something to do with Shakes's disability."

"That's strange," she says. "I would think they'd want him up front near the driver."

"Exit door?" I say. This doesn't make any sense, and Doctor Atwood knows it. Beef and Lamb might have been stupid enough to go for it, but she's not. But for some reason she decides to let it pass. Maybe she wants to see where this will take me, as she always says.

"Wouldn't they want a disabled boy sitting near the driver?" she asks.

"I don't know," I say. "That's what they told Shakes."

I can tell she doesn't believe me. But I'm not lying, really. The reason we got to sit in back *was* because of Shakes's disability. I'm just leaving out the most important part of the story. The part I don't want to tell—that I liked it that way, even though I didn't know why then.

CHAPTER NINE

The first ten minutes of the bus ride were my favorite part of the entire day. I liked sitting there in the early morning quiet, next to Shakes, riding past the forests and over the bridge across the reservoir, the bowl of clear water surrounded by mountains. I liked dozing, dropping off to sleep, and waking up a few miles down the road, with my head on Shakes's shoulder and his head pressed against mine.

At first, it happened by accident, our falling asleep like that. It was so early, we were so tired. I used to get dressed with my eyes closed, opening them only when I had to. I'd stay in bed till the very last minute so I could skip the Joan-inspection of my clothes and my general attitude, and miss her lecture about the importance of the nutritious breakfast that I wasn't eating.

Usually, Shakes and I talked awhile, but pretty soon, we couldn't keep our eyes open. Our heads felt heavy, and drooped. Shakes's shoulder was as good as a pillow. I woke up and realized where I was and went back to sleep again. It was comfortable, we were friends, we'd known each other forever. Shakes must also have woken from time to time, and realized I was there, and drifted off to sleep again, his cheek against my hair.

It wasn't romantic, at least not at first. It was just comfortable, easy. It made me feel as if I had a brother, a real brother, instead of Darling Josh. Shakes and I were like siblings, puppies in a litter. Shakes had a wheezy snore that I totally adored. It had a funny catch in the middle, as if, when he slept, his breath was doing what his body did when he was awake.

We only had those ten minutes of peace, fifteen when the weather was bad and Maureen was too nervous even to drive at her normal slo-mo crawl. We both developed inner alarm clocks that woke us up before anyone else got on the bus. When we slept like that, leaning against each other, we were back in Innocent Little-Kid Land, where you still could do things like hug your friends, regardless of whether you happened to be a girl or a boy. But as soon as anyone else got on the bus, we were in High School Bus Land, where if you rested your head on somebody's shoulder, it meant that you were dating. Two girls could sit like that or walk arm in arm without it meaning they were gay. But I didn't have any friends who were girls. Shakes and Chris and Kevin were still the only pals I had. And now it was mostly Shakes. Already Kevin and Chris were acting a little cool to me, and sometimes it crossed my mind that they felt I'd chosen Shakes over them. Maybe everyone was capable of feeling jealous that way, not just Dad and Joan competing in their minds with Geoff and Mom. Maybe everyone wants to feel that they're the special one who's been chosen.

I liked the feeling of being near Shakes, of just being physically close. If I told Doctor Atwood that, she'd probably point out that I wasn't exactly getting a lot of physical affection at home. And it *was* true that right in the middle of some hellish dinner with Joan, I would escape by looking forward to the next morning, when I would sit next to Shakes.

It was an especially beautiful fall. Everybody said so. The sky was never bluer, the leaves were never more brilliant. And sometimes, half asleep next to Shakes, I'd open my eyes and a dazzling sliver of orange or red would squeeze between my eyelids. Then the slice of brightness would disappear and I'd fall back asleep. Sometimes, I couldn't fall asleep again, but I'd *pretend* to be asleep because it felt so good to sit like that, with my head tucked into the space between Shakes's head and his shoulder. And sometimes I couldn't help noticing that sometimes Shakes wasn't really sleeping, either.

It was a little nervous-making, both pretending like that. It was ever so slightly sexy, though part of me thought it was pathetic. How backward that sitting close to a boy should have seemed like a big deal when there were kids in our grade who, everyone knew, were already having sex. But it *was* a big deal for me. I guess I was socially retarded, and Shakes *was* disabled. So maybe that explained it.

The leaves began to fall off the trees, and, as always, it was sad. It reminded me of how much you can lose overnight. Your family, for example. Even though you thought that everyone was getting along. Your mom could leave as lightly as a leaf falling off a tree. You might not even notice until she was already gone.

The days got rainy and cold, and it felt even better to have Shakes's warm shoulder next to mine.

Every so often, he'd miss a few days of school. Whenever Big Maureen waited outside his house and no one came out and she honked and pulled away, I'd feel something drop down inside me, like some kind of inner parachute. Even when it was sunny, the weather seemed bleak and depressing on those days. Alone in the backseat, I shivered even though the bus was always overheated. And I knew that because Shakes wouldn't be getting on—with his special handicapped backseat privileges—I'd have to find somewhere else to sit by the time the first senior appeared. On those days, I'd save seats for Chris and Kevin, but they always sat together, across the aisle or in front of me, and we didn't talk that much. We all knew I was only sitting with them because Shakes wasn't there.

For the first time, I *seriously* worried about Shakes. What if his health problems were worse than he'd let us think? But then he was back, hopping down his driveway and onto the bus. I knew not to ask him how he was feeling, or why he had been absent.

At first, I thought I was imagining it when things between me and Shakes got more intense. Shakes would be sleeping, or pretending to sleep. He'd turn his head and his lips would graze the side of my neck. Or our heads would both turn at once, and we would be practically kissing. It was strange how, when we were like that, it was almost as if Shakes experienced a miracle cure. He didn't twitch or stutter or spaz. He was completely steady and calm.

By now, those first few minutes on the bus were *really* the best thing about my day. It was better than school, better than after school, when I was mostly home by myself. I'd find myself daydreaming about being on the bus with Shakes. Then I'd snap awake, the way we snapped to attention when anyone else got on the bus.

It was strange, how thinking about Shakes made me feel less lonely, even though I was spending so much time alone that it began to seem a little like my life in Wisconsin, minus Mom and Geoff, plus Dad and Joan and Josh Darling. On weekends, I didn't see my friends that much—not half as much as I used to. Chris was hanging out with Daria Wells.

Most Saturdays, somebody's mom would drive the three guys to the mall. And Daria's stupid girlfriends, with their Minnie Mouse voices, would often come along. It was like some group date with Chris and Daria at the center. Every so often, Shakes would call and ask me to go with them, but I always said no. It made me uncomfortable to be with my friends when the girls were there. It was almost like I didn't know what to be—I wasn't really anyone's friend, and I certain wasn't anyone's girlfriend. It hurt my feelings when I heard they'd all gone somewhere without me, but I told myself it would be better for everyone—especially me—if I pretended I didn't care.

Monday mornings, on the bus with Shakes, I'd say, "Did you have fun over the weekend?"

And Shakes would say, "I don't know. Sort of, I guess." It left me feeling disappointed. Did I expect him to say he'd missed me? That he couldn't have fun without me?

Sometimes, Shakes and I would *really* fall asleep, which meant we dozed through the little time we got to be together. But that was okay, too. I liked having someone I trusted so much that we could leave the conscious everyday world and be back before anyone noticed.

We should have known that nothing that cool and innocent could last. We should have expected the big bust, the scene like the one in the cheesy drama where the couple wakes up in bed and sees the parents or the respective spouses, someone who definitely doesn't want to see them there together.

Sooner or later, we were doomed to be rudely awoken from our happy little backseat dream.

CHAPTER TEN

It was the first of November. I remember because Daria had had a Halloween party the night before, and I hadn't been invited. Shakes was tired from the party, and I was tired because I hadn't been able to sleep. I'd lain awake thinking about everyone having fun without me. Anyway, we were both so exhausted that we sort of passed out. We were all scrunched up against each other, and I guess it must have looked as if we were really making out, our limbs all twisted together in some supertight clinch. And for the first time, we didn't wake up before the others got on the bus.

We awoke surrounded by faces. We opened our eyes just in time to see Beef and Lamb and all their friends looking down at us and making remarks. I felt my own face turn stoplight red. Shakes must have looked as guilty as I did. From the way everyone was acting, you'd have thought they'd caught us having sex in the backseat of the bus.

Gradually, I remembered where I was and figured out what had happened. By now everyone had turned around and was looking at us. They must have been watching us for a long time. I saw a blur of smiling, smirking faces. Only two were in focus. Kevin and Chris were staring at us, as if we were strangers, or as if we were kids they knew and didn't like. I felt as if we'd been taking little baby steps away from each other ever since I got back from Wisconsin, and now we'd each taken a giant step back and nothing could ever fix that.

Chris and Kevin were waiting for us when we got off the bus at school. Daria gave me a huffy disapproving look, as if she'd caught me being a total ho, when the truth is that Shakes and I had done nothing, *nothing*, compared to what people were saying she did with Chris.

"So . . . are you two, like . . . hooking up?" Kevin asked me and Shakes. "Are you guys, like . . . dating? And you didn't bother to tell us?"

"Are you kidding?" I said. "That would be like dating your brother!"

Now Shakes was looking at me weirdly, too, and I knew I'd hurt his feelings. I wondered if he'd been thinking about me the way I'd been thinking about him. And now I'd gone and ruined it.

"Come on," said Chris. "Don't lie. Everybody saw the two of you making out in the back of the bus."

"Man," said Shakes, "I feel sorry for Daria if you don't know the difference between sleeping and making out."

What a brilliant answer! It shut them up for a moment, during which I started to wonder why Chris and Kevin cared so much about what Shakes and I were doing, even if there *was* something going on. Which there wasn't. Chris had Daria, wasn't that enough? But it was as if they thought we'd done something to *them*. As if we'd cheated on *them* with each other. As if *I'd* broken up the four-person gang we'd had since we were little. As if I'd chosen Shakes over them, and they would never forgive me.

CHAPTER ELEVEN

Nothing was ever the same after Kevin and Chris saw me and Shakes sleeping—or making out or whatever they thought we were doing—on the bus. The divide that had separated us when I came home from my year in Wisconsin had widened into the Grand Canyon.

Chris and Kevin acted as if I'd stolen their best friend. That didn't seem right. Another unfair thing was that they seemed to blame me more than they blamed

Shakes. I guess that was sort of like everyone blaming Eve instead of Adam for eating the apple and getting kicked out of the Garden of Eden. I never understood that part of the Bible. Wasn't it Adam's fault, too? But she was the temptress, the evil woman who'd led the fool astray.

I knew it must have been hard for Shakes to be leading a double life. The sweet, tender guy he was with me when we were alone on the bus, and the silent kid who went along with his friends when they acted as if they hardly knew me. Every time I'd go up to Chris or Kevin at school, they'd turn and walk away. Or they'd look at me as if I'd just said the stupidest thing in the world, and then they'd act as if I wasn't there. At first Shakes would seem as if he didn't know what to do, and then he would do what they did. You'd think I would have got used to it after it happened often enough, but I didn't. I couldn't.

I kept trying to understand: Why couldn't they handle it if Shakes and I fell asleep on each other's shoulders? Sometimes I felt as if they blamed me personally for the fact that we all had to grow up and turn into men and women. That we couldn't be little kids anymore. Which didn't seem right, either. I mean, Peter Pan didn't blame Wendy or Tinker Bell for the fact that most kids (except for him) wound up becoming grown-ups.

Sometimes I wondered what would happen if I told Shakes that he had to choose between them and me. Choose between what and what? We never talked about what we did on the bus, and we certainly didn't talk about the freeze-out I was getting from Chris and Kevin. Or about the fact that Shakes ignored me when he was with them.

So of course I didn't tell Shakes that he had to choose.

Which turned out to be the right move. I guess Shakes must have forgiven me for saying that dating him would be like dating my brother. Because our thing in the back of the bus—I still didn't know what to call it—was getting more intense. A *lot* more intense.

Now, instead of just letting his head droop on my shoulder, he'd kind of scrunch up against me with his hands clasped in front of him, almost like paws. I never stopped being surprised by how calm he got when we were sitting like that, how all his tics and twitches disappeared.

On the morning when he first brushed against my chest—when, for the first time, the tips of his knuckles just lightly grazed the side of my breast—he pretended he'd had a spasm.

He said, "I'm sorry, Maisie. Sometimes it's like, I don't know, my hands do what *they* want without asking *me*."

"That's okay," I said. I knew what it was like to feel as if your body were leading you in a direction you weren't sure you wanted to follow. The truth was, I'd liked him touching me. It had felt really good. I knew it was sort of retarded. I mean, lots of kids my age had sex—on TV, and in my school—and here I was going nuts about some guy pretending not to know he was ever so lightly touching one of my boobs. Still, that first time, each of Shakes's knuckles felt like separate electric shocks running down through my whole body. We were still pretending it was an accident, that we didn't know what we were doing.

The second time, he let his hand linger and slightly rotated his wrist so that now it wasn't his knuckles but rather the base of his palm touching my breast. It still could have been accidental.

I guess it was right on the edge between accidental and on purpose. That light touch, that brief contact— who knew? And yet that touch, if it *was* a touch, felt as if it were magically rearranging the molecules, the flow of atoms and particles between his hand and my skin.

Pretty soon, there was no way of even pretending that it was accidental. We were kissing and making out for real, and Shakes was touching my breasts. All that time that he and I were making out in the back of the bus, Shakes must have been under pressure from the other guys because he was still sitting with me and not with them.

I kept trying to imagine what that was like for Shakes, being caught between the guys and me. Later I would realize I hadn't known him as well as I'd thought. But for the moment I really believed that I understood him because we'd grown up together, and then because we took those bus rides together, his head pressed against mine. I must have imagined that personal thoughts were flowing back and forth from one of us to the other. But we didn't know each other at all. I couldn't have imagined what it was like to live inside his body.

It was hard for all of us, figuring out all the weird new stuff our bodies were doing. But it must have been harder for Shakes, since his body wasn't like anyone else's—or anyway, like no one else we knew. His body had always done what it wanted, regardless of what he might have liked. And now he had to get used to it telling him to do even more things he wasn't sure he wanted to do.

For example, touching me. Probably, it would have been easier for him not to. Chris and Kevin wouldn't have resented him, they wouldn't have been so amazed that a kid they'd grown up with—me!—was now a girl who preferred messed-up, twitchy Shakes over perfect, healthy them. I couldn't explain it, myself. Not that they asked. No one could talk about it.

Anyway, Shakes and I thought—or at least *I* thought— that we were safe. After that one time we got caught, we never slipped up. By the time one other kid got on the bus, Shakes and I were sitting bolt upright, and as far from each other as the narrow seat would allow. We were so silent, we sat so straight, we could have been at church.

What we did on that bus was our secret. A secret

that, I guess, we shared with Big Maureen, who must have seen us in her rearview mirror. But, as everyone knew, Maureen was a widow with five kids. She was too overwhelmed and depressed to want to look for trouble. And it wasn't as if we were having sex or smoking or doing something illegal. One of her kids had been born handicapped, too, so maybe she secretly liked to see Shakes getting some low-level action.

On those mornings, with my head next to Shakes's, I felt less like a girl or a boy, and more like . . . well, more like a *person*. That's how close it sometimes felt we were—like two halves of the same creature. Together we made up one normal human being: I was in pretty good physical shape, if you didn't count the oversized boobs. Shakes had the physical problems, but he also had something I wanted and needed, which was a way of looking at the world that was cool and smart and courageous.

I was glad to be his friend, and glad we made out on the bus, and glad for how good it felt when he touched my breasts and we stopped pretending it was accidental.

And then all that ended in one day—one morning, to be exact. I can tell you exactly when. It's all recorded in the papers Joan's lawyer, Cynthia, filed. But even if

I forget it, I could just look up the date of the January senior class trip to Washington.

It was a gray, sleepy morning. A frozen mist rose off the dirty snow, but it was jungly and hot on the bus. Shakes and I dozed off and kissed, dozed off and kissed some more.

After a while, I began to notice that Maureen was driving past the houses where the seniors lived, and she wasn't stopping. And then I remembered they were in Washington for the week, along with the junior honors group that was down in D.C. pretending to be the United Nations. Shakes and I had more time than usual, but even so, it was sad when the bus slowed down and we had to separate and sit up straight.

When the ninth and tenth and eleventh graders got on, they seemed confused. How come the bus was so empty? Then they figured it out. Party time!

Having the older kids off the bus changed the entire mood. All the seats were up for grabs, everyone just sat where they wanted. A seating free-for-all. It was anarchy, I guess you could say, and we liked it. Because for one day, that day, on that bus, we were *free*.

Even though the normal rules were obviously

suspended, the younger kids still couldn't get up the nerve to go for the very last rows. So Shakes and I had the back to ourselves for a while. The seat in front of us stayed empty, and the seat in front of that.

When Chris and Kevin got on the bus, Shakes and I waved and yelled out to them to come back and sit with us.

What an idiot I was! When I think of it now, I feel like some fool saying something friendly and nice and then someone insults her, and she's left standing there with a big friendly smile on her stupid, innocent face.

Chris and Kevin took the seat in front of us. I was so happy, at first. All four of us were together again. It was as if they hadn't decided I was a different person because I had breasts. As if they hadn't made up their minds that they had to stop being friends with me because they'd seen me with my head on Shakes's shoulder. I remembered how it felt in sixth grade when we were the kings of the grade-school bus! It had been so much fun. I was always sorry when the bus rides were over—first when we got to school, and then when we got home in the afternoon.

But it wasn't like that now. It couldn't be. I was

crazy to think we could just travel back in time to the way things were before.

Chris and Kevin sat down. They turned and lightly high-fived Shakes.

Chris and Kevin said hi to me. Not warm or friendly in the least. They were just being polite.

When Daria Wells got on, she runway-walked straight to the back and took the seat in front of them. Chris half stood and leaned over to talk to her. I don't think he consciously knew that he was sort of squirming around, humping the back of the seat. I thought, *He wouldn't do that if he knew how he looked from behind.*

Big Maureen crawled the bus between banks of steaming snow. Chris and Kevin settled down, and after a while they started whispering. I was really curious about what they were saying, because I could watch their shoulders and the backs of their heads get all jumpy and tense and buzzed. They seemed as if they were plotting something, and from the way they kept nodding their heads, I sensed that it was a plot they'd been thinking about for a while.

Chris and Kevin turned around and leaned back over the seat so they were facing me and Shakes. They kept giving each other funny looks, as if they had something to say, something they'd known they were going to say even before they got on the bus.

Maybe they hadn't known that it would happen today, that the bus ride and the seniors' absence would give them the perfect chance. But they'd had it in mind. Motive and opportunity, as they say on the crime shows. They'd been planning to do it sooner or later, and now they were both figuring out it could be sooner. Right now.

Kevin said, "So how about it, Maisie? Can we do it, too?"

"Keep your voice down," Chris said. He didn't want Daria hearing.

"Do what?" I asked.

They laughed. They both looked high. But they weren't.

Kevin looked at Chris. Chris nodded.

"Come on, Maisie. Be fair," Kevin said. "Aren't the four of us old friends, didn't we always divide everything up equally between us?"

"We used to be friends," I was mortified to hear myself say.

"Share and share alike," Kevin said.

I said, "What are you two guys saying? Would you please *make sense*? I don't get it."

Kevin said, "Don't *we* get to touch your boobs? Like Shakes does, every morning?"

Well, *that* wiped the smile off my face.

I looked at Shakes, but he wouldn't look at me. I could feel him twitching like mad. I couldn't believe he'd told them, and even if he had, I couldn't believe he wasn't sticking up for me now. I couldn't believe he was letting the guys talk like that to me. There was so much I couldn't believe, it was hard to breathe, for a second. I probably should have lost it and gone off on them—especially Shakes—right then and there. I should have yelled at them, especially Shakes, *How can you do this?* I could have saved myself a lot of future problems if I'd confronted them right there.

But I was just too shocked, too freaked out.

I looked from Chris to Kevin to Shakes. I told myself: Be cool. Total coolness was never as important as it was at that moment.

"What about it, Maisie?" said Chris.

"Gee, guys," I said. "That's an interesting question. Can I think about it for a minute?"

CHAPTER TWELVE

Doctor Atwood says, "Maisie, do you think we could revisit the incident on the bus?"

"Revisit?" I say. "*Revisit* as in you want me to tell you the story that I've already told a million times because you don't believe me? I thought you were supposed to believe me. I thought that was part of your job."

"I'm not saying I don't believe you," says Doctor Atwood. "Because the fact is, Maisie, I think *you* believe what you're saying happened. But memory's a funny thing. It can distort things. People tell themselves a story about what happened, and they start to believe the story, and then they start thinking that the story is what actually happened. And it becomes the truth. Or *a* truth. Whether it happened exactly that way or not. The mind's a funny thing."

"*Your* mind, maybe," I say.

"Don't be like that," Doctor Atwood says. "I'm trying to help you."

It's something she says so often, I'm almost starting to believe it. "You want me to tell it again?"

Outside the window behind her chair, it's winter, winter, winter.

"Please," she says. "I think it could be really helpful at this point. It's been a while, after all."

"Okay," I say. "If that's what you want."

I'm so bored with the story. I've told it so many times. To Joan and to the principal, to the school administration, and to Cynthia, our lawyer. At first it was hard to tell. In the beginning, it was really embarrassing. But each time, it got easier. And eventually it got boring.

Now I can basically tell it as if it had happened to someone else, to a girl named Maisie who had a bad experience on a school bus. Every time I mean *a girl named Maisie*, I just use the word *I*.

I say, "Stop me if you've heard this before."

"Maisie, please."

"Okay. The older kids were away. Chris and Kevin sat near us. They started saying that Shakes told them I let him touch my boobs, and since we'd been such good friends, it didn't seem fair. I should let them do it, too."

"Why do you think they said that?" asks Doctor Atwood.

"I think they wanted to touch my boobs."

"You know it's more than that, Maisie. You know perfectly well that the boys didn't say that to make you feel comfortable or good. They didn't say that to make you think it was something you might enjoy, something that would feel good to you."

Well, obviously. I didn't think that. But it was better than thinking they wanted to hurt me and make me feel bad. Why would they want to do that? They blamed me for their growing up and for turning into a girl with breasts. Chris and Kevin blamed me for having chosen

Shakes over them. And I still didn't know what Shakes blamed me for. Maybe for confusing him, for making him feel he had to choose between me and Kevin and Chris. But I wasn't the one who'd made him choose. Sometimes I wanted to corner him, and confront him, and ask how he could have done it. But I couldn't bring myself to do it. Maybe I was afraid that I'd get my heart broken all over again.

"What are you thinking right now?" asks Doctor Atwood.

"Nothing," I say. "My mind is a total blank."

"Never mind. Go ahead."

"There's nothing else to say. I told them I needed to think about it a minute. Then I said, 'No.'"

"You said no?" she repeats.

"Yes," I say. "I mean *no*. I said no."

"And then what happened?"

"They looked at each other again. They had it all planned out. Shakes grabbed my wrists and held them down in my lap. Kevin and Chris kind of pawed at my boobs."

"Simultaneously?" asks Doctor Atwood.

"No. First Kevin, then Chris. I think. Or maybe it

was the other way around."

"And what were you thinking about while this was happening?"

"I was telling myself, 'It's just your breasts. It doesn't mean anything really. It's no different than if they were touching your arm. Go ahead, touch my arm if you want.'"

"You detached yourself from yourself?"

"I guess you could say that."

"That couldn't have been pleasant."

"Duh," I say.

"And then?"

"Then they touched my breasts some more. They took turns."

"Were you scared?"

"Of what? We were on the bus! What else was going to happen? Mostly, I was pissed. And then, right in the middle of it, I got so pissed that I yelled really loud, in my nastiest, most sarcastic voice, 'Oh boy, oh boy, that feels really good.'"

"And then?"

"I looked up and saw Daria Wells looking straight at

me, straight at *us*, at me and at the three guys. She was furious. She knew what we were doing. She hated me, and she blamed me. And I knew that she was going to tell."

"Which she did," says Doctor Atwood.

The clock ticks off a few minutes.

I say, "Okay. What part don't you believe?"

"I *do* believe you," she says. "But it just seems so. . . unlikely that your crippled friend would be the one to hold your wrists."

"His names is Shakes," I say. "And he's not crippled. He was the closest to me. It makes sense."

"But he's the weakest," she says. "He'd have the most trouble restraining you. You could have escaped."

"He's not *that* weak." Why am I still defending Shakes?

"And if Daria was Chris's girlfriend, why would she tell the school about something that would get Chris into so much trouble?"

Doesn't the so-called therapist know one single thing about human beings? "Maybe she was just mad. Or maybe for once in her life, she was doing the right thing. Anyway, she *didn't* say that Shakes was holding my wrists. She couldn't have seen it."

"I realize that," says the doctor. Why don't I think she believes me? Am I being paranoid, or is Doctor Atwood a double agent hired to wreck our case?

I say, "There's something else. The money part."

"What money part?"

I say, "Something that happened later."

"What?" asks Doctor Atwood.

'The hour's up," I say. I can hear Phlegm Man in the waiting room. Until now, I never appreciated what a hero the guy really is. I never knew that he could save me.

"Let's start with this the next time. To be continued," she says.

CHAPTER THIRTEEN

My mom used to talk about waiting for the other shoe to drop—waiting for the second bad thing to happen after the first bad thing that's happened. After that terrible morning on the bus, I waited for that second shoe. And somehow I knew that Daria Wells was going to make sure that it dropped. Every time I thought of the expression on her face when she'd seen the guys grope me, I knew she was going to tell someone.

Time goes slowly when you're listening for the sound of that second shoe. When you're expecting trouble. But in this case I was glad for every hour I waited in a state of total dread. Because it gave me some time to think about what I was going to do and say when the truth came out.

Nothing was what I decided it'd be. It had been weird with the guys touching me and all. But there was still a code of honor. These were my oldest friends. I didn't have to rat them out just because they'd touched my boobs. It had been totally uncool of them, totally mean and cruel. Shakes had hurt me so badly, I couldn't stand to think about it. But still I didn't have to go running to the principal and cry like a baby.

Even if Daria told on us, I could just deny it. I could say I'd asked them to touch my breasts. I could say I liked it. Or I could say it never happened, that Daria was making it all up because she was jealous of what good friends Chris and Kevin and Shakes and I were.

For the whole rest of the day of the incident, school was normal, as far as I could tell. No one seemed any different than they usually were. Shakes and I didn't have any classes together, and when I saw Kevin and Chris, they pretended not to see me.

I was trying to convince myself that if everyone pretended the groping incident hadn't happened, maybe that would mean it hadn't happened. Of course, anyone who knew anything about me would have known that something was wrong when, on the bus ride home from school, I sat all the way up front even though, with the seniors still gone, I could have sat anywhere I wanted. When I got on the bus, I noticed that Shakes and Chris and Kevin were in the back row, but I didn't even look at them, not once.

I couldn't help wondering if the guys felt sorry for what had happened, for what'd they done to me and how they'd made me feel. I hoped so, but I doubted it. I was pretty sure that their strongest feeling was fear that I—or someone—might tell on them. It certainly wasn't going to be me. I told myself it didn't matter. Big deal if some guys touched my breasts.

By that evening, I'd pretty much convinced myself that nothing else was going to happen, that the whole problem was just going to go away.

That was when the phone rang. I knew it wasn't for me. No one ever called me anymore.

I was walking through the kitchen when I heard, "Why, Doctor Nyswander!" and I stopped short. It wasn't as if the principal called every day. It wasn't as if the principal had ever called before.

"Why, that's terrible," Joan kept saying, her voice getting higher and sounding so totally stressed and tragic that I thought something *really* terrible had happened. I don't know what I imagined—a school shooting, a kid killed in a car wreck, a school bus crash. It was almost as if I wished it was something like that. Obviously, I didn't, not really. But I knew what the principal was calling about, and I wished it was anything but that.

Finally, Joan said thank you and hung up and turned to me and said, in a totally flat, expressionless—and completely terrifying—voice, "What happened on the bus this morning, Maisie?"

"Nothing. Why?" I said.

"Then what is this about?" said Joan. "Did anyone . . . touch your breasts?"

"Somebody's making it up," I said. "To make me look like a ho."

"Why would anyone want to do that?"

"Boys are always trying to do that. To spread rumors and tell lies and make girls look like hos."

I don't know who was more surprised by what I'd said. My best friends had always been boys. But they weren't anymore. And it wasn't the kind of thing that Joan expected me to say—especially not to her.

Joan paused a minute, then sighed deeply.

"Sad, but true," she said.

CHAPTER FOURTEEN

The next day was maybe the worst, although by this point I've kind of lost the ability to tell better from worse, or even to distinguish slightly better from lots worse. But I've noticed that every time I think, *Things can't get any worse than this*, I can be sure that something will happen that's worse than anything that has happened so far. So let's just say that the next day was a really bad day.

I rode up in the front of the bus again, me and Big

Maureen. I had a seat all to myself. I pretended to be asleep. And I guess I did fall asleep, because the next thing I knew, we were at school.

I walked in the door, and from the minute I entered the hall I heard this funny jingling sound. Everywhere I looked, all the kids seemed to be jingling the change in their pockets and purses and backpacks. It sounded sort of like Christmas, except this wasn't some happy jingle bells, jingle bells, jingle all the way.

The sound had a nasty edge that seemed to be saying, This is about *you*, Maisie. I knew that they were doing it *to* me, *for* me, *about* me. The kids were looking straight at me as they did it. They were sending me a message. Plus, in case I didn't get the point, some really classy guy would shake his pocket and grab between his legs or make believe that he had breasts growing out of his chest, and he'd squeeze his imaginary breasts as if they were those clown balloons that squirt water.

One guy hissed at me as I passed him in the hall.

"Okay," he said. "How much?"

Were the kids saying that I was a whore who had let the guys touch me for money? Was that what Chris had told jealous Daria and what she had told the principal and the whole school?

It hurt me and made me angry, but some part of me felt like it was a sick sort of compliment. The whole school seemed to think that I had the kind of breasts that boys—none of whom, I knew, had gigantic allowances— would pay real money to touch. Okay, it wasn't exactly like making the honor roll or being the class president. On the other hand, I could name a half dozen celebrities, movie stars, and singers who had nothing going for them *but* breasts. And some of them had giant careers. They were probably much richer and more famous than the kids they went to school with, the senior class presidents and honor roll students and so forth. So breasts weren't exactly *nothing*.

Meanwhile, I'd become sort of famous. It wasn't the kind of fame I would have chosen, but still, kids who'd never noticed me before suddenly knew who I was. Everyone seemed to think I had celebrity boobs that guys would pay to touch. I told myself that breasts weren't the only thing I would ever have. They were just what I had now, my special gift that I'd done nothing to earn.

I could live with everybody thinking the guys had paid to touch me. But I couldn't help thinking that there was something else going on—some secret signal that I wasn't picking up on. And there was no one I could ask, no one who would tell me what the kids were doing and saying, what they meant when they made that jingling sound. It was sort of like having toilet paper stuck to your shoe, or spinach between your teeth, and no one will tell you. It didn't exactly make me feel like the giant of self-esteem that Joan always claimed she was trying to turn me into.

Last night, on the phone, Joan and the principal agreed that she would come to school for a two o'clock meeting. It was snowing, but—just my luck—not hard enough to close school early and save me. I kept hoping that the snow would make Joan want to reschedule, but—also just my luck—she had the fancy Swedish SUV. She'd show up in a blizzard, probably hoping that someone would ask her if the roads were bad, and she could boast about her car.

My memory of that entire day is of watching the clock, of waiting for two o'clock to come, and of hearing that constant jingling jingling jingling. It was so bad that in English class, someone jingled, and everyone snickered, and Mrs. Shea said the next person who made a sound or said one word was getting detention. In grade school, I'd *been* that kid, the kid who would say the last word or make the one last sound that sent the teacher over the edge. Now, that part of my life was over. No one would have thought it was funny if I'd fished some coins out of my backpack and started jingling them now.

Finally, it was five to two. Time to go to the principal's office. Mr. Merrill, my social studies teacher, seemed to know all about it. When I held up my hand to be excused, he shut his eyes and nodded.

Joan had wanted a big drama. She'd wanted me to meet her at the front door of the school so she and I could march down the hall like superheroes—superwomen—come to battle for truth and justice. Ever since the principal called the night before, she'd been practically foaming at the mouth. And now she was coming in to save my reputation from malicious lies and slander. I'd told her it would be better if she met me outside the principal's office.

The meeting had been arranged in the way that

Doctor Nyswander said would be easiest for every-one. If necessary there would be a full investigation. Meanwhile, everybody would keep calm and not go bal-listic like Joan. Doctor Nyswander said we would have an open, reasonable, fact-finding conversation, and we'd get to the bottom of what really happened.

Joan was waiting in the hall outside the principal's office so she and I could walk in together, sweeping into the room as we made our dramatic Minnie Mouse–Superwoman entrance.

Doctor Nyswander, Miss Notley, the assistant prin-cipal, and the guidance counselor, Mrs. Blick, were all waiting for us in the office. Doctor Nyswander looked like he was my dad's age, but compared to him, my dad looked like a rock star. Doctor Nyswander's clothes fit wrong, and he wore baggy pants belted under his armpits.

Otherwise there was hardly anything about him dis-tinctive enough to make fun of. The only joke kids told was that he'd been hired because he had the only skill you need to get a job as a principal, which is the ability to walk completely silently and creep up behind kids and nab them for not having hall passes or for cutting class.

Everyone said he'd gotten his doctorate in tiptoeing. They said there was a special store where high school principals buy their shoes. They said Mafia hit men go there, too. They have the same needs in footwear.

Beyond that, there was the icky way Doctor Nyswander said students. *Stoooodents.* As if the word was so delicious, he sucked on it like a Popsicle. I'd laughed at him, along with everyone else. Laughing at the principal was just something you did. Like breathing. But now I almost felt guilty for making fun of him. Every time he said *stoooodents* and everybody snickered, he must have felt like I felt when the kids jangled coins in their pockets.

The principal, Miss Notley, and Mrs. Blick had obviously been talking about me, but when Joan and I walked in, they fell dead silent. That didn't exactly give me the most comfortable feeling, and it certainly took the drama out of our grand entrance. I had to remind myself that no one had been hurt or killed, that all these adults had gotten together and were looking tragic just because some guys supposedly touched my breasts on the back of the bus—which I was going to deny, anyway. Then I remembered that Shakes had been one of them, and I must have looked tragic, too. Which made them feel they had to look even more serious, and sadder.

Doctor Nyswander stood and shook Joan's hand and then mine. The principal stared into my eyes. He was going to get to the bottom of this—starting, I guess, with me.

"Thank you both for coming in," he said. As if I had any choice. He was doing everything in his power to seem supercollected and calm. But I kept noticing droplets of sweat percolating up from behind his tie and leaving dark blotches around his collar.

"We can't thank *you* enough for taking this seriously," said Joan. "If someone's spreading lies about Maisie . . ."

"We take it very seriously," said Miss Notley, and the principal and Mrs. Blick nodded.

Joan said, "My husband—Maisie's dad—would have liked to be here with us. But he's performing an emergency root canal."

"Poor thing," said Miss Notley. It was hard to tell if she meant my dad or the poor patient having the root canal.

"Terrible weather we're having," said Mrs. Blick. "I

hope the roads weren't too bad."

"Oh, no. No problem. I've got a Volvo. It handles marvelously in adverse weather conditions," said Joan. Everyone stared at her for a moment, then looked at their hands.

"Please sit down," said Doctor Nyswander. They'd brought two chairs in for us. The principal closed the door.

After a long silence, Miss Notley said, "Maisie, one of the reasons I decided to attend this meeting was in case it made you feel more comfortable to have only women present. Doctor Nyswander can step out of the room, and it will be just the two of us and Mrs. Blick. And, of course, your mom."

"Stepmom," I said.

Miss Notley smiled sympathetically at Joan as she said, "Stepmom. Of course."

I said, "It's fine with me if Doctor Nyswander stays. I mean, is it supposed to, like, make me die of embarrassment if I have to say the word *boob* in front of the principal? Or what?"

The adults looked as if *they* were going to die of

embarrassment. But what did they expect? Did they think I'd just stand there like Hester Prynne and let them make me wear the letter *B* for *Boobs* on my chest? I was still the same person, the same kid who'd go right up to the scary house on Halloween, the one who'd say the last word to push the teacher over the edge. Did they think that person had disappeared just because she'd grown breasts? All at once, it struck me: These people had never known that other person. They'd only known the girl with big breasts. Joan had known me back in the day, but Joan had a short memory for anything that wasn't about Joan, and Joan had forgotten who I used to be.

Now Joan said, "Maisie, dear. Please be calm. We know how hard this must be for you."

"Exactly," said Doctor Nyswander. "Which is why we *all* need to keep calm. Perhaps then . . . Maisie, you could tell us in your own words what happened?"

Who else's words did he *think* I would use? I said, "There's nothing to tell. Nothing happened."

Mrs. Blick said, "Dear, denying it won't mean it didn't happen."

I shot her a furious look.

"Denying what?" I said. I had the strangest feeling—detached, somehow. As if I were watching myself in a movie. *Maisie in the Principal's Office*. Or, *Maisie Versus the Adults*. I had to admire the girl playing me. She was gutsy and cool and smart.

The principal said, "Yesterday morning, a *stoooodent*, one of your classmates, came to my office in tears and made some pretty serious accusations."

"Like what?" Of course he'd told Joan what Daria had said, but I wanted to hear it from him. "Like who?"

"Never mind who," he said, as if we all didn't know. "This was reported in strictest confidence. She . . . I mean the *stoooodent*, said there had been an inappropriate incident involving you and some boys in the back row of the school bus."

"It never happened," I said. "Nothing . . . *inappropriate* . . . happened." I told myself that what had happened wasn't *inappropriate*, it was just creepy and weird. I didn't like lying, but it seemed important, even necessary. And at that point I still had the fantasy that if I covered for Shakes and Kevin and Chris, they'd apologize for asking to touch my breasts and would tell me they still cared about me. That they didn't know what they'd been thinking, they hadn't meant to hurt my feelings. First I'd give them a hard time, but after a while I'd forgive them, and we could go back to being friends again, or anyway whatever we were before the incident happened.

Miss Notley said, "Maisie, why do you think a student would tell us such a disturbing story if it wasn't true?"

I said, "Because Daria Wells is a big fat liar. Because she's jealous that I'm such good friends with those guys. She's jealous because I've known them longer than she *ever* will. Those kids and I have been friends since we were babies."

When I said *Daria*, the name sort of sat there for a while, in the middle of the room. What about *strictest confidence*? I wasn't supposed to know. Time stopped for a moment, then started again.

"*Exactly* what did she say happened?" I finally asked, when the silence became unbearable.

Miss Notley said, "Well . . . borders were crossed."

"Like the U.S.–Mexican border?" I said.

"This isn't a joke, dear," said Joan.

"It certainly isn't," agreed Mrs. Blick.

I said, "You mean the border around my boobs?" Oops. I didn't want to sound like I knew what they were talking about if I was going to pretend that nothing happened.

The three school officials sighed, deeply and at once, and Joan sighed, too, as if she was imitating them.

"Maisie," said Doctor Nyswander. "We're not accusing you of lying. We understand exactly why you might not want to talk about this."

"About what?" I said.

More sighs, all around.

Joan said, "We all know how rumors get started. Especially in the student population. I've seen many youngsters in my practice who have been hurt by cruel whispering campaigns. And frankly, if Maisie has no memory of this, it's a little hard for us to figure out where all this could possibly be coming from—"

I jumped when Doctor Nyswander cleared his throat in a way that sounded like the bark of a big, nasty dog. It shut Joan right up.

He said, "We took the liberty of speaking to the boys who were accused. Er . . . implicated."

"Separately or together?" I asked.

Miss Notley said, "Separately. Of course."

"And?" said Joan.

"And," said Doctor Nyswander, "all three of them admitted it rather quickly."

Did they torture the truth out of them? Did they keep them without food and water in nasty cement-block interrogation rooms and play good cop–bad cop? I looked at the three school officials facing me, practically melting into little puddles of stress, and somehow I couldn't imagine a scene like that taking place.

"This is outrageous," said Joan.

Doctor Nyswander said, "You need to remember that your daughter—"

"Stepdaughter," I said.

"—that Maisie isn't the one being accused. She's the innocent victim."

"I'm not a victim," I said.

Mrs. Blick said, "None of us want to think of ourselves that way. Especially if we have experienced abuse."

Joan said, "Maisie, did any of your fellow students touch you in a way that made you uncomfortable in the back of the school bus?"

"I already said no."

Miss Notley said, "Did they touch you at all?"

I said, "No. Except that one of them put his arm around me because I was cold. I asked him to. Is that against the rules?"

Mrs. Blick said, "That's all that happened?"

I said, *"Nothing* happened. How many times do I have to tell you? I don't care what they said. They were probably scared or something."

"If they hadn't done anything, why would they be scared?" asked the principal.

I just looked at him. Hadn't the guy ever heard there were innocent men on death row? I thought, I have to talk to the guys! They were probably worried that I'd crack under interrogation. And they'd wanted to tell their own version before I could tell mine. When they hear that I'm refusing to talk, they can just say they made it up because they were afraid that people would believe Daria. When they hear I've denied everything, they'll be so grateful for my being a stand-up kid that Shakes and I—

Doctor Nyswander stopped me in midthought. He gave me another of those searching soul-to-soul looks. Then he looked away. He walked to the window and gazed out at the snow. When he spoke again, he was still looking out the window, as if this was all just too horrible to say to the actual people in the room, and he preferred to say it to the thick, forgiving snow.

He said, "There's another detail that, painful as it is, we, I think we should mention . . . just to clear the decks, so to speak. To open the windows and let the air in."

It was sort of funny, him standing at the window and saying that. But still, I didn't like the sound of it.

Joan said, "Fine. Let's hear it. If lies are being told about Maisie, we should know what they are."

Miss Notley stared down at her long, thin hands, clenching and unclenching her fingers. When she thought no one was looking at her, Mrs. Blick switched off her hearing aid.

The principal said, "We do know how rumors get started and then spread like wildfire through the *stoooodent* population. So there's probably no truth to this, either. But I feel that you should know."

Yikes, I thought. *This must be nasty. Nobody can bring themselves to even say it.* The principal and the assistant principal and the guidance counselor kept looking at each other. At the end of their silent conference, Miss Notley had been picked.

Miss Notley said, almost in a whisper, "Apparently, some students have been claiming that after Maisie let the boys touch her, after she basically *asked* them to touch her, she said that it had felt really good, and she asked if they knew anyone who would pay her to fondle her breasts."

"Who said *that*?" I asked.

The school officials looked at one another. No one wanted to go near this. Miss Notley whispered again, "Well, I suppose it would have had to have been the boys themselves. The boys who are . . . involved."

Joan said, "That's absurd. Absurd. Absurd!"

For the first time ever, I was glad that Joan said something, even if she said the same thing three times in a row. I'd lost all that cool detachment, that feeling of watching myself in a movie. I felt like I was having one of those dreams where you scream and scream and no sound comes out. Pure fury boiled up inside me and cooked everything else away.

All the times I'd been angry in my life—at my mom leaving, at Geoff for acting like a spoiled brat, at Joan practically every minute I was around her, at my dad for not sticking up for me, at Chris and Kevin for abandoning me and treating me like I'd grown a whole new head instead of just boobs—all that swirled together and boiled hotter and hotter. I could feel a fire blazing under my eyes when I thought of those lying slobs saying I'd asked if other boys would pay to touch me. How could they say that? We used to be friends! I'd thought that Shakes really liked me. Had Shakes said it, or just the other two? I didn't want to ask.

I understood the jingling coins now. All the smirking and whispers and jingling money was suddenly, disgustingly clear.

Joan said, "What kind of young woman do you think my husband and I have raised? I don't want to hear another word of this unless my husband is present. And, just possibly, our lawyer."

Lawyer! The magic word that Doctor Nyswander most dreaded hearing.

"No," he said. "I didn't mean . . ." And now *he* could hardly talk.

For some reason, they all swiveled around to look at me. I heard that jingling sound again, but now it seemed to get louder and louder. The inside of my head felt hot. Steam seemed to be filling my brain and all the cavities in my skull. What would they do if steam actually came hissing out my ears?

How could the guys have said that? Did anyone believe them? Could anyone really think that I was some slutty freak, some cheap ho who got off on letting guys pay to touch her? I could hardly stand to think about the fact that the guys who said this weren't some weird pervert strangers I'd just met. These were my oldest friends, the buddies I'd known my whole life.

I know that I could never be a suicidal person, but if someone had come along at that moment and said, *Just jump out that window, Maisie, and you won't have to feel the way you're feeling, you won't have to get through the next couple of days. Jump out the window and you won't ever*

*have to face Chris and Kevin. And Shakes. Or the other kids
at school. You won't have to decide what you're going to say
when you see them*—well, it might have been tempting.
But I wasn't going to jump. As bad as this was, it wasn't
worth killing myself. And besides, to be perfectly practi-
cal, the principal's office was on the first floor.

I wasn't going to do anything drastic. I was just
going to have to get through this. I would just have to
stay cool and wait for the moment and get revenge,
not big revenge, just something to even the score and
make me feel a little better. If that was possible. Which
I doubted.

I'd think that and calm down and then get furious all
over again. I was in full-blown outrage mode when I felt
myself starting to shake like an overloaded appliance,
like a dishwasher or washing machine that's on the edge
of imploding. I needed to get out of there, out of that
office, out of that school. Fast. Right now.

I said, "Joan, could I talk to you? Outside."

The others were talking quietly. But something
about my tone of voice sliced right through their polite
little chatter.

Doctor Nyswander told Joan, "Perhaps we can check

in later on the phone." He meant he expected me to tell Joan everything—the truth!—and Joan would tell him everything I told her. But that wasn't going to happen.

"Perhaps," said Joan. "And perhaps I'll have my lawyer call you." For a minute—a few seconds, really—I almost wanted to high-five her, until I told myself that Joan just felt *she'd* been insulted, and, as far as Joan was concerned, it didn't have all that much to do with me.

As Joan and I walked out the door, I heard Mrs. Blick mumbling something about how she'd send more notes around to my teachers so I wouldn't be marked absent for the rest of the afternoon.

"Thank you," Joan remembered to say. "That's very thoughtful of you, Mrs. Blick."

I didn't say a word till we got into Joan's car and were a couple of miles from school. A battle was going on in my head, between the force of reason and the force of sheer rage. And rage kept winning out. How could the guys say something like that? When I felt the anger get stronger, it felt weirdly like losing an arm-wrestling contest. There was something restful and sweet—almost a relief—when you finally gave in and let the person pull

138

down your arm. I had every reason to be furious and no reason to want to protect my friends—none of them, not even Shakes.

The windshield wipers were making a racket. Slog slog, groan, and creak as they pushed aside the heavy, thick sheet of wet snow that followed them halfway back across the window. I was glad we were in the car. It was always easier to talk when you didn't have to look at the person.

I said, "Joan, I need to say something. It's not exactly true that nothing happened on the bus."

"I figured that," said Joan.

Meaning what? Meaning that she was lying all that time she'd claimed she believed me? It was too confusing to try and figure *that* out now, especially when Joan was saying, "Maisie, I just want you to know that nothing you can say will shock me. People do . . . unusual things all the time. Especially when their hormones are pumping, and they don't know how to read the new signals their bodies are sending. I've seen that so often in my practice. Especially young people your age. They're always experimenting. There is nothing you could have done, nothing you could have said—"

Nothing *I* could have done? Wait a second! *Wait a second*! Did Joan mean she thought it could be *true* that I had wanted the guys to touch me and had asked if they knew anyone who would pay me to touch my breasts? I tried not to sound angry. I tried to stay controlled.

I knew I had to sound scared and hurt. I was faking it, I had to. But what made it more believable was that I wasn't faking it completely. Anyway, I was saying exactly what Joan expected and wanted to hear. She could have made it up herself. She hardly had to listen.

Nor did I have to work that hard. In order to get a catch in my voice—that wobbly, wounded tone—I just had to think about Shakes or Kevin or Chris, one of them, or all three of them, deciding what they would say if Daria told and they got caught. Maybe Chris imagined it would make Daria stop being angry at him for whatever she thought she saw the four of us doing at the back of the bus.

Maybe the guys thought that saying that would get *them* out of trouble. This was more than my saying yes, more than yes meaning yes. This was please, please, it feels so good, and by the way, can you find someone to pay me? That would make me so despicable they'd look like total innocents.

How could that *not* make someone mad? How could that not hurt a person? I wanted to tell Joan to pull over and stop the first hundred people we passed and tell them the story and ask: If this happened to you, how would *you* feel? But there weren't a hundred people on the streets of our town. And certainly not in a snowstorm. There were more than a hundred kids in our school, but I could hardly ask them. I thought about it, and thought about it, and I felt tears come up behind my eyes and leak down into my throat.

I said, "It was the day of the senior trip. So we pretty much got to sit wherever we wanted on the bus."

Joan turned the radio down and sat up straight. I could tell she was being patient until I got to the good part—the part about touching and boobs.

"At first I thought they were just kidding around. And I kind of went along, even though it wasn't exactly my favorite subject."

"What wasn't your favorite subject?" said Joan.

"My breasts and the guys touching them," I said.

"Had this gone on before? The boys asking to touch your breasts?"

I took a deep breath. If I said yes, it would be the first big lie. They'd only asked that one day.

"Yes, they had," I said, and waited for lightning to strike, or the sky to fall. But nothing like that happened.

"So this was repeated behavior? *Repeated* harassment?"

"They *kept* on saying it," I told Joan. "But they wouldn't stop joking, until someone—probably Kevin or Chris—came out and asked me if they could touch them that day. That day the seniors were away on their trip and we were all sitting in the back of the bus."

"Which one of the boys asked first?" asked Joan. "You're probably going to have to remember."

A chill went through me when she said that. Maybe I'd seen too many cop shows. Once more, I imagined my friends being held in separate interrogation rooms, only now they were really scared, and some sex crimes detective was tricking them into incriminating themselves. *Give it up*, the cops said. *Your buddies have already squealed.* For a moment, I came really close to telling

Joan the truth. Then a voice in my head said, *Hey, have you heard about Maisie? She let three guys on her bus touch her boobs. And she'll do it again for money.*

"Joan," I said. "Can I have some time? I have to think about it more."

"Okay," said Joan. "Take as long as you need."

The voice in my head spoke up again: *Maisie asked her friends to find guys—like, customers!—who would pay to grope her!*

I said, "They all three asked me at once. They all three asked to touch me."

"All three at once?" Joan sounded a little dubious, and I couldn't blame her.

"Well, not *at once* at once," I said. "But they were all asking."

"What did you tell them?" said Joan.

"I looked at Shakes, but he wouldn't look at me. I just wanted them all to calm down. When they asked if they could touch me, I said, 'That's an interesting question. Can I think about it for a minute?' I thought they were joking. I couldn't believe they were serious."

"And then?"

"And then they asked again and kept asking. They begged and pleaded for a while, and I started getting nervous, because I could tell they meant it. I remember looking around . . ."

"And then?" said Joan. I wished that she would stop saying that. I felt like *I* was the one being interrogated.

"I said no. Definitely no."

"And then?"

"I don't know. That part went on for a long time. I decided to ignore them. I looked out the window, but every time I'd look away, one of them would say something like, 'Come on, what about it, Maisie?'"

"What happened next?" asked Joan.

"Well, it was sort of strange, because right after it happened, I had the feeling they'd planned it. Because it went so smoothly. One of them glanced at the other, then they all exchanged these looks."

"And then?"

"And then suddenly, Shakes pinned down my hands. He kind of leaned into me and held me so I couldn't move. I struggled a little, but I couldn't do anything. I couldn't defend myself or fight back. And the other two kind of pawed and mashed my breasts all the way to school. It *hurt*."

"Oh, you poor thing." For once, Joan sounded genuinely sympathetic. "And what did *you* do, Maisie?"

"I told you," I said. "I said no."

"I mean, while it was happening."

"I zoned out." Well, this part was true, at least.

"Why didn't you scream or cry for help?"

"Because it was all so embarrassing. I didn't want the embarrassment to get any worse. I thought if I just kept quiet and let it happen, it would be over, and that would be that."

Joan nodded. This seemed to be in keeping with what she'd heard and read, maybe even what she'd come across in her practice. Typical victim reaction. Part of the story had been easy to tell, because it was the truth. They did touch my boobs, and I did zone out. The hard part was the lie about Shakes holding down my hands.

Joan said, "And then they made up that awful lie about you wanting to charge others money. Honestly, I think those boys should be expelled. I think we should receive an apology from them and from the school. I think we really might have a case here. I'll have to talk to Cynthia and see."

"Cynthia?"

"My friend. She's a lawyer."

Suddenly, I was filled with dread. Pure dread. It felt like icy water trickling down my back.

Joan said, "It would be a matter of principle. Something we would be doing—a fight we would be fighting—for you and all the girls like you who are the innocent victims of boys like that."

"I'm not a victim," I said. "And they're not boys like *that*."

"Then what *are* they like?" asked Joan.

I didn't have an answer. Or if I did, it was way more complicated than anything I could have explained to Joan. For a second, I felt sorry for Shakes and Chris and Kevin. Maybe they *had* been fooling around and it just went too far.

"What if I don't want to fight?"

"We'll support you," Joan said. "But someone needs to draw the line. Girls can't be treated this way."

Then I thought about the guys saying that I wanted

them to find other boys to pay to touch me.

"Fine," I told Joan. "Whatever."

Just as we pulled into the driveway, Joan said, "I have to go and get Josh now." She hesitated, then said, "Maisie, do me a favor. Let me decide how we're going to present this situation to your little brother. I'd like to have a certain degree of control over how we handle the information. Not that you should feel you've done anything wrong or that there's anything to be ashamed of."

"I don't," I said. "I understand. Tell Josh whatever you want to."

I knew that telling Dad would be harder than telling Joan. It was hard enough for him to accept the fact that I *had* breasts, let alone breasts that boys would want to touch. He'd known Chris and Kevin and Shakes since they were little kids.

Joan made Dad come home early from work. I thought of all the people with raging toothaches left to suffer in agony because my dad needed to hear how some kids had groped me on the bus.

In the end, I couldn't bring myself to tell him. And that was pretty weird, too. It was as if my dad and I had also crossed over to opposite sides of the line that separated girls from boys, the divide that forced men and women into separate bathrooms, separate dressing rooms, separate conversations. I asked Joan to tell Dad. Who knows what she said. I no longer cared. The two of them called me into Dad's study. It felt like being ordered to go to the principal's office, all over again.

Dad said, "Maisie, is this true? Did those boys do that to you?"

I nodded. This time it seemed more likely that Shakes *must* have held down my hands. How else could it have happened? How could I have just spaced out and let the guys do that to me?

"Oh, you poor poor sweetheart," said Dad. "Come and give me a hug."

I went over and hugged Dad. And it made me sad all over again. It was the first time that I was aware of my breasts between us. And I couldn't help feeling that my dad noticed it, too. He couldn't wait for the hug to be over. He was relieved when we separated and he could just pat my back.

CHAPTER FIFTEEN

Cynthia, the lawyer—*our* lawyer, as Joan keeps saying—
is Joan's good friend. It's easy to understand why.
They both have that same brassy, in-your-face quality.
They both have their I-am-woman-hear-me-roar thing
totally down.

They both like to think of themselves as alpha
females, so it's kind of funny that Cynthia's office should
be so totally alpha-male-lawyer: leather-upholstered

chairs with metal studs, dark bookcases filled with dark books. I always think that if you took down any of those superimpressive leather-bound law books, they'd be hollowed out inside, and they'd contain some secret stash, like Cynthia's face cream and diet pills. Or maybe her hormones and steroids. Cynthia wears tight little T-shirts so you can see she's really buff, and sometimes, during our "meetings," I catch Joan staring enviously at Cynthia's biceps.

A few days after the incident on the bus, Joan called Cynthia to set up our first meeting. But so many kids must be suing their school boards—or so many people must be suing *somebody*—that it was another few weeks before we could get an appointment. I've never been able to tell if the whole lawsuit thing was Joan's idea, or Cynthia's. Probably, they put their perfectly coiffed, perfectly salon-streaked heads together and cooked up the whole thing.

I was already bored with the story by the first time I told it to Cynthia. And she seemed bored by it, too. Or maybe that was just how she always listened, because listening meant that she had to wait until it was her chance to talk.

After I finished, she asked Joan, "How long after the incident did the school call you to report it?"

"That night?" Joan says. Why did she say it as if she was asking a question? And why was Joan asking *me*?

"That's right," I said. "The same night."

Cynthia looked disappointed. Positively crushed.

"Glad to hear it," she said. "For Maisie's sake, I mean. On the other hand, it's not the greatest thing for us. From a purely legal standpoint, these cases work out better if a certain amount of time elapses before the school admits wrongdoing or negligence and decides to take action. Actually, I'm not surprised. Don Nyswander's wife works for Calder and Smitt. So he's pretty legal-savvy. It was pretty smart of him to call you as soon as he realized there was a problem. The longer a school delays about that, the smoother these cases have gone."

"Which cases?" I said. I wanted to know if what had happened to me had happened to other kids. Was Cynthia saying that the country is full of girls whose best friends groped them on the back of the school bus and then lied and said she wanted to charge other guys to do the same thing?

"There are precedents," Cynthia said. *Precedents*, as

it turns out, is Cynthia's favorite word.

"Like what?" asked Joan.

"Well, the Supreme Court handed down a ruling saying you can sue a school when the harassment is so serious and sustained that it violates a child's right to an education. The parents of a fifth-grade girl, in the South somewhere, brought a case against a fifth-grade boy who'd been . . . well, actually, he'd been touching her breasts."

Wow, I thought. *How does she know that? Cynthia's been doing her homework.*

She said, "The girl reported the incident, but the school didn't do anything for a while—*anything* in this case meaning taking action to get the boy suspended or expelled."

"We don't want to get these guys expelled," I said.

"It wouldn't be the worst thing," said Joan. "It would certainly send a message—"

"I'll deny the whole thing," I said.

"It's just as well," said Cynthia. "Those he said–she said cases are often extremely tricky. In any event, the key words here are *critically indifferent*. We have to prove the school has been critically indifferent. Which is going to be a little hard to prove seeing as how Don Nyswander called you that same night."

Joan said, "Well, other things have happened since then. And the school has done nothing about it. I think the legal term might be . . . *a pattern of harassment.* Or . . . *a hostile atmosphere.*"

"Excellent," said Cynthia. Then she turned to look at me, and her eyes went all gooey. "Maisie, dear, I can imagine, or maybe I *can't* imagine, what it's like to keep having to go to school with the boys who did this to you."

I said, "You can't, actually."

"Maisie," warned Joan. "Be polite and appreciative, won't you, dear? Cynthia's doing this as a favor to me. On a contingency basis."

"I just meant she couldn't imagine," I said.

"I understood what Maisie meant," Cynthia said.

I said, "Are we going to get a ton of money if we win?"

Cynthia sighed. "Kids these days. Where's their innocence? When I was their age, no one sued. A child would simply not have known that."

"They watch TV," said Joan, and she sighed, too. "They know everything negative about out society. They know how low things have sunk, and it doesn't even seem low to them."

Cynthia and Joan fell silent, both so worried about "kids these days" that for a moment they seemed to forget that I, an actual kid, was actually in the room. It was as if the two of them had slipped into some kind of dream.

"How much could we get?" I asked.

Cynthia was the first to awake from the dream. "Let's see what happens," she said.

"Are the boys who assaulted you present in the court-room?"

"Your Honor, I object to counsel's use of the word *assault*."

"Objection sustained."

"Are the boys who *molested* you present in the court-room?"

"Objection, Your Honor. *Molested* is inflammatory."

"Sustained."

"Are the boys who *touched you inappropriately* here today in the courtroom?" In the dream, I know that the person asking me is supposed to be Cynthia, Joan's lawyer. *Our* lawyer, as Joan keeps saying. But the lawyer in the dream doesn't look like Cynthia, exactly. The lawyer in the dream reminds me of a certain late-night news anchor with the frozen, scary face who never smiles or blinks, and whose name I can never remember.

"Yes," I say.

"Can you identify the boys who touched you, Maisie?"

I look over at the crowded table where Shakes and Chris and Kevin sit with their lawyers.

None of them will look at me. I'm trying to send Shakes a message. But it's not getting through.

"Will the witness answer the question—"

I open my mouth. I wake up. But this time, I wake up screaming, "*No!*"

"Maisie? Maisie? Are you all right? Is something wrong?"

It's Joan, knocking on the door. I can't believe I'm

hearing her shrill birdcall voice, first thing in the morning. I lie in bed, wishing that I could figure out how to get back into the nightmare about the court hearing. As bad as it was, it was better than the nightmare of getting ready for school, and then going to school, and facing the nightmare—the waking nightmare—that's waiting for me there, for months.

Still, I'm glad to be awake, so I can tell myself that the stuff in the dream isn't really happening. We're suing the school board, but we're not putting my three former best friends on trial for sexual harassment or assault or whatever Joan wanted to charge them with in the first place. Joan would still like to get the boys expelled, but that's not going to happen, I don't think. The school is taking a "wait and see" attitude until the case against them gets settled.

"I'm fine," I say. "Nothing's wrong."

"See you at breakfast," Joan chirps.

So I've started the day with a lie. Something *is* wrong, starting with the prospect of breakfast with Joan. And I am absolutely *not* fine.

I don't look in the mirror as I get dressed. The last

thing I want to see is my bare chest, the breasts that caused all this trouble. I put on my jeans and favorite blue sweatshirt, no words, just plain navy blue, size XXL.

Before all this happened, I used to wait in my room until the very last minute, until I heard the school bus honking. Then I'd go racing out the door, leaving Joan ranting about the importance of the five food groups and eating a healthy nutritious breakfast.

"Tomorrow," I'd say. "I promise. But I'm late. Big Maureen's waiting."

"Don't call her Big Maureen," Joan would say. "That's unkind."

"Size-challenged Maureen," I'd whisper under my breath.

These days, I have all the time in the world to sit there and pick at every revolting morsel that Joan puts in front of me. Because I've stopped taking the school bus. Joan and Cynthia have decided that I'm too "traumatized" to ride the bus. So Joan drives me to school every morning.

Joan looks at my sweatshirt and jeans and sighs

dramatically, as if I'm causing her some deep personal pain.

"You know, Maisie," she says, "for me, one of the most tragic things about this unfortunate situation is that it's making you hate your own body."

"I don't hate my body." I'm certainly not going to tell Joan how I've figured out how to get dressed without even glancing in the mirror.

Joan sighs again, going for even more drama. "Look at how you're dressed! You might as well be wearing a big trash bag over your head."

So Evil Stepmom has momentarily trumped Sitcom Mom and Doctor Joan Marbury, Therapist.

I want to say, *Why don't you look at what you're wearing?* Joan is dressed the way she thinks I should be dressed, as if to give me the idea. Her jeans are too tight, her heels too high. Her makeup's so thick, you can practically hear it cracking like ice on a pond, and she's wearing a really expensive black jacket with a fake—or is it real?—fur collar.

"I dressed this way before. I've always dressed this way," I tell Joan. "It's comfortable. Nothing's different. What's *your* problem?"

Joan decides to ignore my tone. "Why don't we go to the mall this weekend and buy you something pretty?"

Nothing could sound worse than going to the mall with Joan and letting her nag me into buying something that looks crappy on me and that I'll never wear. And besides, someone might see me. The kids in my grade hang out there. God, what if I ran into Kevin and Chris and Shakes, and Daria and her friends, one big happy gang? And there I would be, totally miserable, all alone with Joan the Wicked Stepmom.

Joan says, "I'm not the Wicked Stepmother, Maisie. I need you to believe that."

It creeps me out when she says that, as if she knows what I've been thinking. The last thing I need is to broadcast every thought so loud that even Joan can pick it up on the airwaves. Could I have called Joan that when I was talking to Doctor Atwood? I can't be that paranoid. I have to trust Doctor Atwood. Sort of.

"I *don't* think that."

"Don't think what?" Joan's going to make me lie again.

"I don't think you're the Wicked Stepmother."

"Good," says Joan. "Believe me, I'm not. I'm trying,

I'm really trying, Maisie. I wish you'd make an effort, too."

"Where's Dad?" I say.

"Your dad had an early patient. What a saint your father is!"

She's right. My dad's a good guy with bad taste or bad luck with his wives. But it's true that he's scheduling patients earlier and staying at the office later, probably so he'll miss the latest episode of the Joan versus Maisie throwdown. Tons of people suddenly seem to need root canals at eight in the morning. Who can blame him for wanting to avoid the daily fight that starts with Joan firing off some passive-aggressive insult and my refusing to answer. The strange thing is, I know she sees the whole thing differently. She's told me that she's *reaching out*—the phrase makes me want to throw up—and *I'm* being passive-aggressive.

It takes the whole breakfast to get down a mouthful of Joan's supercrunchy granola. Especially while she's watching.

She says, "Have you and Doctor Atwood discussed your diet? You've hardly eaten any of your cereal. I'd hate to think you want to punish your own body for what those boys did to you."

"I eat plenty," I say, the truth for once. "I'd eat a lot more of this cereal if it wasn't so much work. Chewing it burns more calories than I get from eating it. I need somebody to prechew this crap for me."

"That's disgusting, dear," says Joan. "Josh loves granola. Don't you, darling?"

On cue, Josh Darling enters the room, fresh and scrubbed from the shower. What normal nine-year-old boy showers without being forced to? He pours himself an overflowing bowl of sandy granola and chows the whole thing down, like one of those Guinness World Records freaks who do stunts like eating cars.

"Time to go!" Joan announces. Another benefit of this new life is that Josh Darling gets a ride to school. Might as well—Joan's driving. Josh hates it, too, but he won't say so.

As his reward for keeping his mouth shut, and because he's Joan's actual darling son, Josh Darling gets to sit up front, and I ride in the back. Before she and Dad got married, Joan leased a red Toyota Camry.

The pathetic sporty divorcée car with the child-friendly safety rating. Right after the gross wedding at Ye Olde White Bread Inn, my dad bought Joan the Volvo SUV so Joan can play soccer mom and make the other soccer moms jealous.

Your stepmother's a trophy soccer mom. That was something Shakes used to say. Remembering it makes me feel better, then instantly worse.

As always, Joan spends the whole ride to school trying different ways to start a conversation. She tries this, and if it doesn't work, she tries that. It's beyond annoying. Every time a pop star gets into trouble or punches out some paparazzi or goes into rehab, Joan tells us all about it. She acts as if it's fascinating girl-gossip, but I know it's a warning: Don't drink or smoke or take drugs, eat right, and don't get violent. Half the time, the people she talks about are celebrities I don't even like, or I used to like but don't anymore.

Joan says, "What about that girl singer, what's her name, shaving her head and getting all those tattoos? Isn't that appalling?"

Silence. Not even Josh Darling is taking the bait. So

Joan turns on the radio and talks along with the news, giving us her fascinating views on every foreign and domestic situation. I've learned to screen out Joan's voice. I don't want to form my opinions about the world just so they're the opposite of Joan's. I slump down in the backseat and put my hands over my ears.

"Maisie?" Joan's been watching me in her rearview mirror and making exaggerated motions when she talks so I can read her lips in case I happen to be deaf or can't hear her over the radio, which in fact I hardly can.

"What's the matter now?" Joan's not only the thought police, she's the gesture police.

I take my hands down from my ears. "Nothing," I say. "Just thinking."

A contradiction, obviously. Something *is* the matter: I'm thinking ahead—to school. I'm wondering what new hell is waiting for me when I arrive.

I can't believe it's only been a few months since the whole thing erupted. How amazing that, in such a short time, I seem to have developed all new magic powers. I've become Magic Ice Cube Girl. Everyone freezes when they see me. In fact they make a big drama of freezing, like kids playing Statues or Simon Sez or some other baby game no one's played for years. Then they do these big stagey double takes and sneer at me and go back to whatever they were doing or saying before they saw me.

It's almost like something they *have* to do, even the ones who have mixed feelings about my so-called case, even the girls whose moms—Joan's friends—have been told they're supposed to *support me*. Giving me the freeze-out is almost like a ritual they're required to perform. When they see me, they're like people touching a rabbit's foot or some other lucky charm. I've become their lucky charm. Or maybe their unlucky charm. I'm the one everyone hates, I'm the one who makes the rest of them feel closer to each other. Even the nerdiest kids give me poisonous looks, trying to hide their joy because I've taken their place at the absolute bottom of the ladder of social success. I know that they feel really good about that. So at least I make *someone* happy.

Among the halfway sensible things that Doctor Atwood says is that I shouldn't pity myself, that this part of my life won't last forever. My dad and Joan are looking into private schools in the area, so maybe I can start over with all new kids who don't think they know everything about me. But I'd probably have to leave the state to really be able to start over and besides, there's only one private school in the area. It's mostly for faculty kids from the local Ivy League college. I couldn't get in there anyway. My grades aren't that great, and I don't have any special talents.

And I certainly couldn't get in now. I mean, hey, I'm just the student everyone wants—the girl who's suing her former school. So I'm not likely to transfer soon, unless Dad and Joan ship me off to some super-expensive boarding school

Homeschooling is not an option. At least Joan and I agree on that. So for the time being—as Doctor Atwood keeps emphasizing—*for the time being*, Joan drives me, every morning, straight into the heart of the nightmare that school has become.

Three months might not sound like all that long, but the last three months seem to have taken forever. I've learned a lot in that time—for example, I know what it must have been like for the first person who came down with the bubonic plague, or a leper in the Dark Ages. When I walk down the halls at school, I should probably ring a bell, the way sick people had to go around warning everyone out of their way. Except that I don't *need* to ring a bell. Everyone knows I'm coming, and they move aside and make way, except for the occasional shove, the accidental elbow that comes scarily near my breasts. I've learned to keep my arms crossed.

Practically every day, Joan tells me that if kids are mean to me, or if I experience bullylike behavior, I should tell her immediately, and she'll tell the school administration. And if they don't take immediate action, it will strengthen our case against them.

Everything should be documented, says Joan. Everything is evidence, proof for our side. Of course, it *is* being documented—stored up in my mind. But my only satisfaction comes from not weakening or telling Joan a single bad thing that happens.

This morning, when I walk into school, I have the definite sense that something has changed. Nothing's better, of course, just different. I can sense it in the way that other kids look at me, in the charged excitement I can feel in the air. It's as if they all know a secret about me, and it's taking all their willpower not to let me in on the secret.

As I'm going up the stairs on my way to homeroom, I hear someone say, "Maisie, are you okay? Don't you need to go to the *bathroom*?

That's how I know that it—whatever *it* is—is waiting for me in the bathroom. Are the kids planning to beat me up? I don't think they'd do that. There aren't a lot of fights in my school. The parents go nuts about stuff like that. Most of them want their kids to go to college. Fights don't look good on our record, and there's some kind of zero-tolerance policy. Automatic suspension.

Maybe some kids have drawn or written something nasty about me on the bathroom walls or stalls. That's a pretty common form of communication. Bathroom graffiti is sort of like the school newspaper, except that more kids read it than read the school paper, and the only stories that get reported are about which girl is a ho and what couple had sex at which party. It's strange how everyone believes what they read on the bathroom walls, even though—only now it occurs to me—it might be completely untrue.

Well, whatever is waiting for me in the girls' bathroom—the beating or the nasty graffiti—neither option makes me eager to go find out. On the other hand, some part of me wants to see, so at least I won't be in the humiliating position of having the whole school know something about me that I don't know. I imagine the kids spying on me and vying for the privilege of being the first one to see the look on my face when I come out of the bathroom.

I decide to get through the day without going to the bathroom at all, but the whole thing makes me so nervous that I *really* have to pee by the end of English class. I spend the last ten minutes of class crossing and uncrossing my legs and wondering if peeing in my jeans would put me in a better or worse situation than I am in already. Worse, no doubt about it. I hold out through one more class period. Then I can't take it anymore. In the middle of social studies class, I raise my hand—with everyone watching—and get a hall pass and leave the room.

I could swear that even the hall monitors know

what's going on. But they pretend not to see me, and no one even asks to see my pass.

I convince myself that no one's planning to bash my head in. People have better things to do than hang around the smelly bathroom, waiting for me to walk in. It probably *is* just something written on the wall. So what? What do I care? Sticks and stones, et cetera.

I inch open the door, just in case someone is there. Just as I'd thought, the bathroom is empty.

I see the drawing scrawled on the tiles, and for a half second I'm relieved. It's going to make me feel like crap, but at least it won't (physically) hurt. It takes me another moment to comprehend how *big* the drawing is. It's huge, it's monumental, it's more like a mural. It takes up the entire wall between the sinks and the stalls. Why didn't someone report this? Why hasn't some friendly janitor come in to remove it?

The first thing I see is the word *Maisie*. It gives me the chills to think that someone was thinking about me as he or she (probably she) scrawled my name. Above my name is a figure that I guess is meant to be me. She's naked, though it's hard to tell, because she's just a stick figure with a head and two humongous naked boobs. Oh, and a stick arm that extends straight out from her stick body, holding bunches of money, bills marked with dollar signs.

A balloon mushrooms out of the ugly face, supposedly mine. And inside the balloon are more letters, which say, *How much?*

For a split-second I think I might actually throw up. At first I'm just embarrassed, but then anger gets all mixed in with shame. I reach into my backpack for the little digital camera Joan gave me and instructed me to use in case I needed to document some new incident of harassment. She never really specified what sort of incident that might be, but this is one, and I know it. I take a picture of the drawing, then another, then another. Then I put the camera away and go into a stall.

Joan is waiting for me in the Volvo, parked where everybody can see. I've begged her to wait for me around the corner, but she won't. She says she likes watching kids play in the school yard. But I think she really wants to have everyone admire her car. Which just proves how out of it Joan is. She thinks a high school kid's dream car is the Swedish Sitcom Mom van that goes from zero to sixty in ten minutes.

Not that Joan would ever take it up to sixty. Or anyway, not with me and Josh on board. Who knows what she does when she's alone, speeding around on the back roads and listening to Fleetwood Mac with the volume blasting.

"How was school?" Joan sings out as I approach the car.

"Crap mostly," I say.

"Please don't say *crap* every other word."

"Please don't correct me before I say two words."

"You *said* two words. Oh, dear. Maisie, would you mind terribly getting in back? We have to pick up Josh, you know."

"Sure." What was I thinking? I get in back, which is fine. The farther away from Joan, the better.

I can't believe that I'm the one who starts the conversation. But the snapshot I took in the girls' bathroom feels like it's burning a hole in my backpack.

"How's the case going?" I say. "Have you talked to Cynthia?"

"Slowly," says Joan. "But it's going. According to

Cynthia, the school should be doing something more. A hostile atmosphere exists, and it's the worst possible thing for your education. That's why Cynthia feels we have a solid case when we charge that you're being denied your right to an equal education."

"Whatever," I say. "I need to change schools."

"I know that," says Joan. "And you will. But let's sit tight for the moment."

"How much money could we make from the case?" I ask. "If we win."

"Honestly, I don't know," says Joan. "Fifty thousand, maybe. There haven't been that many cases like ours. And there's a chance we could lose. But it's not about the money. It's really not about that. It's about principle, about treating women with respect, about our right to control what happens with our bodies. You know that, Maisie, don't you?"

"What will we do with it?"

"With what?"

"The money. If we win."

"We've talked about this," Joan says. "It's for you, of course. Tuition. The very best boarding school.

Anywhere you want. And, of course, somewhere where you can get in."

Wicked Witch, I think.

"Your dad and Josh and I will really hate to lose you. We'll miss you so, just like we did when you went to Wisconsin. What a mistake that was!"

"Tell me about it," I say.

"But I promise you, we'll find somewhere you feel safe, somewhere cool."

I doubt I'd like any school that Joan thought was cool. But the so-called cool boarding school has to be better than living with Dad and Joan and going to a school where everybody hates me.

I say, "I've got something to show you."

Even Joan is smart enough to hear the seriousness in my voice.

"Can it wait till we get home?" she says.

"I don't want Josh to see it," I say.

"Oops. Good thinking," says Joan. "What a thoughtful, caring older sister you are!"

Joan drives for a few blocks, then parks on a quiet street of neat lawns and colonial houses.

I hand Joan the camera.

"Press the button," I say.

Joan squints at the screen, then shuts her eyes and shakes her head.

"Oh, you poor dear," she says. "This is exactly the sort of thing that needs to stop right now. *Right now*! Meanwhile, it's *evidence*. The school needs to put its foot down. Like I say, this isn't about the money, Maisie. This is about justice."

The next day, Joan prints out two copies of the photo. She gives one to Cynthia and hands me the other copy in an envelope when she drops me off at Doctor Atwood's office.

I open the envelope, and my stomach lurches.

"What are you giving me this for?" I can't believe she's made me look at it again.

"'Mention it to Doctor Atwood," Joan says. "Just mention it, Maisie. See what feelings it brings up."

"I know what feelings it brings up," I say. "Misery. Nausea. Rage."

Joan pretends not to have heard me. "That's what

therapy's for. I think Alana should see what you had to see. I think she needs to know that."

"Shouldn't that be *my* choice?" I ask.

"Of course," says Joan. "Of course it's your choice. But I think she needs to know what you're going through. And one picture is worth . . . you know."

I don't want Doctor Atwood to see it. Maybe I don't want to talk about how much it hurt my feelings. Suddenly, I'm panicked about bringing the envelope in with me, and her asking me what's inside, and having to tell her the truth. I wish I could ditch it, but where?

There's a little foyer just outside Doctor Atwood's office. But I can't leave the envelope there. You leave by a different door. I can just imagine Phlegm Man opening the envelope and getting an eyeful. I have to bring the photo into the office with me. It feels weird to be carrying an envelope in which there's a cartoon of me, done by someone who hates me, showing me as a tiny head with stick arms and legs and a giant pair of boobs.

The thought of it makes me so mad that I want to

help Joan win this case. I want the school to pay.

I spend the first twenty minutes of the session looking at my watch.

"How's school?" Doctor Atwood asks.

"Fine," I say.

Then there's a ten-minute silence, for which Dad and Joan are paying.

At the end of it, Doctor Atwood says, "Are you going to tell me what's in the envelope?"

"Nothing," I say. "It's a paper I have to hand in for school. I thought I'd check it over while I was waiting for you."

Doctor Atwood looks at me. I hope the expression on her face doesn't mean she's learned to tell when I'm lying.

"About what?" she says. "What's the paper about?"

"*The Scarlet Letter*," I say.

"How appropriate," she says.

"Outrageous, right?" I say. "How typically insensitive to make me sit in a class where the kids are discussing *that* book, of all the books in the world." I'm so offended by the thought—because now I'm the shunned

Hester Prynne, the one the whole community thinks is a slut and maybe even a witch—that I almost forget I'm lying. It takes me a moment to remember that we're actually *not* reading it for school. I read it last year, in Wisconsin, when it was still safe to read a story like that and not take it personally.

I'd rather think of *The Scarlet Letter*—as I recall, Hester was a lot better than people gave her credit for, and in fact she was a really good person who just made one mistake—than think about the photo inside the envelope: supposedly my head and my boobs, and definitely my name, on the wall of the girls' bathroom. I don't want Doctor Atwood to ask how it makes me feel, as if the answer isn't so obvious she could figure it out herself. Though maybe I would like to ask her what she thinks of a stepmother—an adult—who gives her stepdaughter a copy of a nasty drawing of herself and tells her to show it to someone. Even her shrink.

"Actually," Doctor Atwood says, "it's the perfect book for a person in your situation to read. It makes you realize how often the whole community can be wrong, and how crucial it is for the individual to believe in herself and her basic goodness and—"

I say, "Can I ask you something?"

"Within limits." Doctor Atwood gets annoyed when I interrupt her.

"What would you call someone who believes that if she drives a certain kind of car, the whole world will worship her and want to *be* her and want to drive the same car she drives?"

"An American," says Doctor Atwood.

"Ha-ha," I say. "Very funny." Which it is, sort of.

Then she asks, fake-casually, "What kind of car?"

"A Volvo SUV," I say.

"I see," says Doctor Atwood. She thinks, then says, "Maisie, I'm not sure that it's going to be productive for you to ask me to judge your stepmother. I'm on your side, as you know, and I'll do anything to help you get along better with Joan, but—"

"Okay, okay," I say. "Forget Joan. New question. What do you call a person who thinks she's the only human being in the world and doesn't care what anyone else thinks or who they really are, and she just wants everyone to be like her?"

Doctor Atwood is all smiles today. This one is an I-give-up smile. She knows I'm still talking about Joan. "Technically speaking, I suppose you'd call a person like that a narcissist. You know who Narcissus was, don't you, Maisie?"

"Sort of," I lied.

"Better brush up on your Greek myths, dear."

"Wait a second. I like Greek myths. Okay. Wait. Wasn't he one of those people who got turned into a plant?"

"A flower, actually," says Doctor Atwood. "And why?"

"I forget."

"Because he couldn't stop looking at his own reflection in the water."

It takes me another few seconds before I say, "I get it." And now a smile breaks over *my* face. Doctor Atwood is totally onto Joan. It makes me feel I can tell her more than I've been revealing. But still, I'm not ready to trust her with anything important.

I say, "So what do you do if you happen to have somebody like that in the family?"

She considers this for a while, then says, "You try to be sympathetic. You try to get stronger so that person can't hurt you. And you do everything in your power not to become like that."

"Good answer," I say.

CHAPTER SIXTEEN

It's the Saturday after I found the drawing of myself and "forgot" to show the picture to Doctor Atwood. It's one of those good news–bad news days. The good news: No school. The bad news is the danger that Joan will insist on taking me to the mall.

In fact, Joan has my whole day planned. There *is* a trip to the mall. A little shopping. Then two hours of what she calls "Joan time," which basically means ditching me and Josh at home and going to the gym, or maybe to get her nails done, or her hair streaked. Josh and I are supposed to read in the living room and promise we won't move.

Then, at three, Dad's getting off work, and we'll split up into our real families: Joan and Josh, Dad and me. Dad and I will do some father-daughter-bonding thing. Go grocery shopping. Big deal. Or maybe we'll go to an afternoon movie, which would be okay except that it makes me think that this is the low point to which my teenage life has sunk. Two trips to the mall on Saturday, each with a different adult.

It's the usual torture with Joan. We're not just going shopping, which would be bad enough. But it's worse. We're supposed to be having *fun*, with a free side order of self-esteem-building for me.

After Joan tells Josh, a million times, to stay where he is and not go anywhere and not talk to any strangers until we pick him up, we drop him off at the video arcade. You'd think Joan might be more paranoid about cutting loose a nine-year-old kid in a mall full of perverts, but the difference between the way Joan treats

Josh and the way she treats me is that she actually lets Josh do things that might make him happy.

The arcade would make *me* happy, compared to shopping with Joan. But it wouldn't make me *that* happy. It's a place I used to go with Chris and Kevin and Shakes. I'd just as soon avoid it now. If I was going to run into them, that's probably where it would happen. I'd get there just in time to watch the three guys showing off on the machines while Daria and her stupid friends looked on and made admiring coos and squeals. I tell myself it's too early for kids to be here. But I'm still on edge.

Joan flits from store to store like a large, inappropriately dressed butterfly fluttering from flower to flower. In every store, she makes a beeline for the thing that would look absolutely the worst on me, and that I would feel weirdest wearing—the ruffled shirts, the cheerleader skirts, the see-through blouses with lacy matching T-shirts underneath. Joan holds them up to my sweatshirts and jeans and tells me how gorgeous I'd look. At least the mall isn't crowded yet. It would be so much more humiliating if anyone saw Joan and me playing this sick little game.

"Do you need underwear?" Joan asks.

Wicked Witch, I think. "No thanks," I say. "I've still got tons I bought with Mom."

If she says I need a new bra size, I'll simply have to kill her.

It helps a little to think about my narcissism conversation with Doctor Atwood. I imagine Narcissus gazing at himself in the lake until he turns into a flower and doesn't even notice the difference. When Joan looks in the mirror, she sees herself, and when she looks at me looking in the mirror, she sees herself. I'm out of the equation, an innocent bystander at the major love affair that Joan is having with Joan. Which is a relief, in a way. It lets me come home from the mall with a sweater and a skirt I will never wear, but without having been too horribly insulted by Joan's free fashion advice.

Sitcom Mom Joan takes me and Josh home and waits about five seconds before rushing off to go have her Joan time. She spends those five seconds setting me and Josh up in the living room with our books and telling us, "I want to see you here when I come back. I want you each to have read at least two chapters."

Josh and I wait till we hear her car pull out of the driveway. Then we turn on the TV. Joan could have blocked the satellite, if she was serious. But she doesn't care that much. Basically, she just wants her Joan time, and she doesn't want any trouble.

Insanely, Josh thinks he can grab the remote. I'm the oldest, it's my house. Every rule of kid etiquette says it's mine. But the weird thing is, I let him. I'm so tired from my terrible week. I'm not going to fight with him like I fought with Geoff, Mom's so-called grown-up husband. I'm so exhausted, I'm just as glad to lie on the couch and watch whatever Josh wants to see.

Josh goes straight for MTV. Wait a minute. Shouldn't a kid his age be all about the Disney Channel? And it's not only MTV. It's one of those *Girls Gone Wild* shows. Same drunken frat kids, same blond girls lifting their shirts, the fuzzy buttons dancing on them, dancing along with the girls, and everybody screaming and yelling until the shirts come down again. That's what Josh wants to watch? He's nine! What's going on here?

Of course, I can't stop thinking of that time I went to Shakes's house, when I came back from Wisconsin, and they were watching one of those programs. I should have taken it as a warning, I should have gone home that minute. They'd become different people. They'd turned from kids into boys. But I'd refused to see that. And ignoring it broke my heart.

"I can't believe you're watching this crap," I tell Josh.

"I wish you didn't say crap all the time." He's imitating his mom, and we laugh. I like him better already. It's not his fault he's Joan's kid and she likes him better than me. After all, she's his real mom. He's the one who's got to deal with her all his life. Meanwhile, he's watching this program that's all about drunk girls showing their boobs. I feel like it's my duty to set the poor kid straight.

"What does this program do for you?" I can hear my voice rising. "What does it mean to you, Josh? Is *that* who you want to be? One of those guys? Going to islands where poor people live and getting smashed and screaming till some poor girl shows you her tits?"

Poor Josh! The kid is staring at me. He must think I've lost my mind. Well, he's right. I'm blaming him for everything that isn't his fault. I'm acting like he's one of the drunk guys yelling at the girls, or like he's the one who produced the show—or as if he's done what my so-called friends did.

Josh says, "Is that what happened to you? Did those guys yell and scream till you showed them your boobs?"

Wow. I'm not prepared for this.

"No," I say. "Not really. Those girls are drunk. They don't know what they're doing."

"Did you?" says Josh. "Did you know what you were doing?"

I shake my head. "Let's stop right here. I don't want to talk about it, okay?"

There's something about the way he's looking at me, with his head cocked, like a puppy. He's not trying to be cute, he *is* cute. And I've just had that moment of liking him, of thinking he's not so bad and feeling sympathy for the poor kid.

I can't bring myself to lie to him.

Which makes things a little complex. Because I'm no longer sure what's a lie and what's true.

I remember two things happening, two things that

were sort of like each other, but that weren't each other.

Those two things have one thing in common, the one fact that no one's denying. And it's this: Chris and Kevin and Shakes all touched my boobs in the back of the school bus.

The question is how it happened. You could say there are several versions of the same event. And that's not counting what I said at the beginning, and that I was planning to keep saying—namely, that *nothing* happened, and that Daria made the whole thing up because she was jealous of me and my friendship with the guys.

If you don't count the nothing-happened story, the first version of the incident is very complicated. The second version is very simple. And then there's the version in which money comes into the story.

I told Joan the simple version, and then I told it to everyone else. For a while I remembered the first two versions of the story together. Then it began to seem as if the second version, the simple one, was the way it happened. And then the money thing got added into the mix, and I sort of went into free fall.

It's weirdly hard to sort them out, the story and the

truth, even though I was physically there, an actual eye-witness. More than an eyewitness. I was actively involved. The victim, says one version. A ho, says another. So you might think I would know. But the only thing I understand now, which I didn't know before, is how confusing it can be. I mean, the whole question of what's true, what's a lie, what you think, what you say, and what you start to believe.

"What do *you* think happened?" I ask Josh. "What have you heard?"

I can't blame Josh for not answering. On screen, a blond girl is pouring a whole pitcher of beer down the front of her T-shirt.

"Weird," says Josh. "I don't get it. I mean, what's the big deal about boobs? Why isn't it sort of the same as letting somebody touch your arm?"

First I think, *Is Josh gay?* Then I remember: He's a kid. He hasn't turned into a guy yet. He doesn't even know that he's not supposed to be honest.

"It's not the same as your arm," I say. "But I don't want to talk about that now."

"What do you want to talk about?" asks Josh.

"Shut up for a second," I say. "I need to think."

The strange thing is that, the whole time they were touching me, I kept telling myself, *Relax, it's no different than if they were touching your arm.* Not that I even wanted them touching my arm, at that point. Besides which, it wasn't true. It *wasn't* like they were touching my arm. My breasts are the newest and tenderest part of me. My arms have been around for my whole life, they've had time to toughen up. And it hadn't felt the same when Shakes touched my arm as when he touched my breast.

Josh gets bored pretty soon, and we watch the last hour of *Spirited Away*. We have the television off and our books open long before Joan returns.

Dad comes home an hour after he said he would, which pretty much kills the possibility of an afternoon movie. But here's the really spectacular treat: Dad has to get an oil change!

Joan says, "Why don't you go with your dad, Maisie? Keep each other company." There's no way for me to refuse. It would make my dad feel worse, and he already looks like a guy who's been doing root canals since eight

A.M. Well, he'd better keep doing as many as he can. Who knows what fancy ride Joan will want after she realizes that no one else but her thinks the Volvo is hot?

Part of me knows that my problems aren't Joan's fault. What happened with Shakes and Kevin and Chris didn't have anything to do with her, unless you count the fact that I would never have left for a year to live with Mom and Geoff if Joan hadn't been so annoying. If I hadn't left, maybe it would have been different. The guys and I would have seen each other changing, day by day. It wouldn't have seemed so major. And maybe Shakes and I would never have started doing that stuff we were doing in the back of the bus, which pissed the other two guys off so much that . . . so much that they did what they did. So if you want to look at it that way, you could say that *everything* that happened has all been thanks to Joan.

I can tell that Dad would prefer to get the oil change by himself. Probably he'd like his equivalent of Joan time. Dad time. He probably needs it after a week of poking around in people's mouths, and listening to Joan. But he doesn't want me to feel rejected either, and so—two potential rejects—we keep each other company. Just like Joan tells us to do.

I know Dad's practice does pretty well, but I also know he's not exactly one of those celebrity cosmetic dentists-to-the-stars you read about in magazines. Dad's still driving his high-mileage Saab, while Joan's out there tooling around in the brand-new fully loaded Volvo. Well, fine, that's Dad's choice, too.

We get into the Saab and start out for the oil-change place. If you looked at us, you'd probably think that we're going to pay some kind of tragic hospital visit. We feel the pressure: We're *supposed* to have a conversation, which is bizarre, because those long-ago, pre-Joan days, we'd always just been able to *talk*. I don't remember what we talked about, I just know that we did.

It freaks me out that my dad is the only other person who remembers that time. The only one who was there with me during the years with Mom. Shakes and Kevin and Chris knew Mom, but now they're out of my life. There are hardly any living witnesses to corroborate my story that once I had a real family like the other kids on the block.

Doctor Atwood once said that the real reason I'm so mad at Joan is because I'm mad at Mom, but that I'm afraid of *those* feelings. I refused to talk for the rest of the session, and the next time she brought it up, I said I'd stop coming to therapy unless she shut up about it. So I guess it means she's probably right.

Meanwhile, every time Joan forces me and Dad to spend some quality time together, I make a special point of bringing up Mom. That may be another reason that my dad doesn't want me along for the oil change. Which makes me feel even worse, which makes me not want to be with him, either. And that makes me feel so guilty that I'll say anything to break the uncomfortable silence and make my dad feel better.

I say, "How are things in the office, Dad?" Then I zone out while Dad drones on about some shadow on some poor dude's X-ray that only he noticed, and it meant a whole complicated surgical operation, and if my dad hadn't picked it up, the guy's mouth would have exploded.

Poor Dad! This has got to be hard on him. And

I don't mean the oil change. I mean the incident, the court case, the whole scandal and drama. It's probably tough for fathers to think about their daughters kissing some guy. Let alone about some guy touching her breasts. Let alone three guys touching her breasts. Let alone whatever Dad thinks went on in the back of that bus.

Oddly enough, considering what *I've* been thinking, Dad says, "This can't be an easy time for you, Maisie."

I say, "You're kidding, Dad, right?" For a moment he looks at me as if we actually do know each other from before everything got so complicated.

He says, "I hope you know you can talk to Joan about all of this."

So we *don't* know each other. If we did, he'd know I *can't* talk to Joan. Maybe he's just telling me he'd rather I not talk to *him*. Let's go back to the subject of root canals. Something pleasant and safe.

I say, "Dad, didn't you like it better when Mom was around and we could all just relax and not have to think of ourselves as a *family* doing *family things*?" I can hear myself start to imitate Joan. I hope my dad doesn't notice. Or maybe I hope he does.

"We tried that," says Dad. "We tried it your mom's way. It didn't work."

"So what went wrong?" I'm surprised to hear myself say.

Dad's surprised, too. He keeps his eyes on the road. "I remember your mother saying it was hard to be a woman."

"What did you say to that?"

Dad says, "I'd say that it was really hard to be a human being."

"You can say that again," I tell him, and he laughs. They're both right. But maybe my mom was more right. I'm the one with the breasts, I'm the one whom no one in school will talk to. I'm the one who's being blamed for everything.

Dad says, "I still think it's hard for everyone. Male and female. But apparently your mom didn't agree."

At the oil-change place, I wait in the car until the garage guy asks me to get out, and then I find Dad in the waiting room. We sit on either side of the coffeemaker reading car magazines. Then we get in the car and go home.

Sitcom Mom is bustling around the kitchen. "Did you two kids have fun?"

Two *kids*?

"Tons," I say.

"Yes," says Dad. "It's always fun to go out with my favorite daughter." He sounds a little robotic, but so what? Joan laughs anyway.

"Darling, do me a favor," she tells Dad. "We've completely run out of milk. Could you run down to the grocery?"

Dad practically races out the door, he's so happy to get away.

Ten minutes later, the phone rings. Joan answers, and I can tell from the look on her face that it's Mom. Dad and I were just talking about her, so it's almost as if we're in touch, even though we aren't. But I don't want to talk to her now. Somehow I have a bad feeling about the conversation she wants to have.

"No, he's not here, Jeanette. I'm sorry. Want to talk to Maisie?"

As Joan hands me the phone, she makes a major lip-synch drama out of the words, *It's your mother.*

I shake my head. Closing her eyes, Joan hands me the phone.

"Oh, hi, Mom," I say.

"Hi, darling," says Mom.

"How's Geoff?" I say.

Mom laughs. "Is that a trick question?"

"No," I say.

"In that case, he's fine," says Mom.

There's a silence, and I know. Somehow, Mom's found out.

After the incident happened, and then after it all blew up, I made a conscious decision not to tell Mom, and I asked Joan and Dad: If it was okay with them, could we leave Mom out of this for a while? My dad was a little uncomfortable about it, but Joan couldn't have been more thrilled. She must have thought I'd finally realized whom I could trust and confide in.

I don't know why I wanted to keep it secret from my mother. Maybe I didn't want to worry her, or make her feel worse about herself than she already did. It wasn't her fault, and—as I couldn't help noticing when I'd been in Wisconsin—she had enough to deal with, being married to Geoff.

Or maybe I was afraid that she'd try to talk me into moving back to Wisconsin. In a way, it would have been the most sensible solution, getting away from a school where everyone despised me and back to one where they just ignored me.

But for some reason, I would have felt as if I was giving up, giving in—as if I'd been defeated. And Wisconsin had been boring. Whatever it was, my life at the moment wasn't boring. I wanted to hang in there— at least long enough to find out what was going to happen, and how my own little drama would end.

At the same time, I knew that my mother would eventually hear the truth. After all, she was my real mom—eventually, she'd pick up something on her real-mom radar. And now, it seemed, she has.

After a silence she says, "Marian called me."

I say, "Marian as in Shakes's mom Marian?"

"Marian as in Marian," says Mom. "Maisie, what the heck is going on? I want to hear it from you first before I talk to your father and Joan. I want to hear your version of the story. I need to know what's happening. I can't believe I've been left out of the loop for *months* about something this important. Maisie, you're my daughter. Can you imagine how I felt when Marian called me and I had no idea what she was talking about? How do you think it made me look?"

"Mom," I say. "This isn't about you." I think about Narcissus gazing at himself in the water. Maybe Joan isn't the only one. Maybe Dad has a weakness for women like that.

"I know that," says Mom. "I'm not upset about *me*. I'm worried about *you*, darling. What happened between you and Shakes? You were always such close friends. It was always so cute to see the two of you together."

"That was then. This is now," I say.

"What's now?" asks Mom.

"It got cuter, and then it got less cute."

"Maisie," says Mom. "Could you *try* to make sense?"

"I *am* making sense. But never mind," I say. "What did Shakes's mom tell you?"

"Well, she says there's a . . . discrepancy between your story and Shakes's account of what occurred."

"So are you saying I'm lying?" I realize I'm holding my breath.

"Not at all! Not at all! Why would you think I'd think

that? Of course we believe you. And we'll support you, dear. We're behind you all the way. But I need to hear it from you. I want to hear your version."

I pause for so long that Mom says, "Maisie, are you still there?"

"I'm here," I say. "It's just that, the funny thing is . . . well, that's the same question everybody seems to be asking me all the time."

"And the answer is?"

"Believe it or not, Mom, the answer is . . . I don't know."

"How could you not *know*?" asks Mom.

"Gee," I say. "That's an interesting question. Can I think about it a minute? Can I call you back later?"

"I don't understand," says Mom.

"I promise," I say. "I'll call you back. I need to think for a while."

CHAPTER SEVENTEEN

"Are the boys who assaulted you present in the court-room?"

"Your Honor, I object to counsel's use of the word *assault*."

"Objection sustained."

"Are the boys who *molested* you present in the court-room?"

"Objection, Your Honor. *Molested* is inflammatory."

"Sustained."

"Are the boys who *touched you inappropriately* on the school bus here today in the courtroom?"

Chris and Kevin won't look at me. But Shakes does, and we stare at each other.

"Will the witness answer the question—"

I try to speak. Nothing comes out.

And then, as always, my eyes blink open, and I wake up with the judge's voice echoing inside my head.

So that's pretty much where we are now. Every couple of nights, I have the same dream, a dream like the cheesy ending of the cheesiest TV crime show. The final courtroom showdown moment. The witness contradicts herself. Then she bursts into tears and, through her sobbing, cries that she doesn't remember what really happened. The defense lawyer rushes the witness stand, demanding to know how she can tell one story, then another, and not know which one is true. When I used to see those scenes on TV, I'd think: *Sure. Right. No way. She knows how it happened. She just doesn't want to say.*

So I guess that's one difference between life and TV.

Because now that it's happening to me, I can actually see how you could remember two ways in which something happened, and how you could lose the ability to tell which story was true. First you think it happened one way. And then you think: *No, maybe not . . .*

The fact that I keep having the dream seems a little strange. For one thing, Cynthia has promised me that I won't have to appear in any kind of court. Because of my age and so forth, and the delicacy of the situation, they'll just take a deposition. So I'm going to be spared that. I'm not going to have to see—not even once, in real life—what I get to watch in perpetual reruns in my dreams.

Doctor Atwood says that the dream isn't strange at all. It's only natural that I feel responsible and guilty, even though none of it is my fault, and I need to remember that.

Every time Joan talks to Cynthia, the case seems to have ramped up instead of simply going away, which I still keep hoping it will. Cynthia says that it's *critically indifferent* of the administration to leave the boys in school, where I have to see them every day and where they have the opportunity to harass me again. Cynthia keeps insisting that the school suspend the three boys, as a "gesture of good faith," but so far the school has refused to do that. I think that Cynthia secretly wishes they'd feel my breasts some more. Because she's told us that our best chance of winning is if the harassment is severe and pervasive—and the school does nothing to stop it. That's why Joan gave me the camera and told me to document stuff like the drawing of me on the bathroom wall.

You'd think the school would cave in and give Cynthia whatever she's asking for. But Doctor Nyswander seems to think that it's a matter of principle. He must believe I provoked the guys into touching my boobs, and then had second thoughts and felt guilty, and turned on them. And he's not going to make them suffer.

Apparently, he brought up *The Crucible*, and the Salem witch trials. Big Mistake. That sent both Joan and Cynthia totally over the edge into blind raging fury. Was Doctor Nyswander accusing them—and me—of being hysterical raving *female* witch-hunters? In fact, everything that happens seems to make Cynthia and Joan even angrier and more determined. So they've reached a kind of standoff. Joan says the school board is digging in its heels, that they're circling the wagons just the way the male power structure always does when anyone challenges their authority.

Anyway, the result is: I get to see Shakes and Kevin and Chris every day. I see them, but they just look right through me as if I'm not even there. I can't blame them for not wanting to be friends with the person whose lawyer would love to get them expelled from school with giant black marks on their permanent records.

The fortunate thing in all of this—if you could call anything fortunate—is that now the other kids pretty much leave me alone. You'd think a bunch of normal high school kids would keep on teasing and torturing me, but no one does. They practically scatter when they see me coming down the hall.

Doctor Atwood says they might be scared to come near me. She says that once you start getting lawyers involved, everything changes, and people get nervous; they start watching their backs. Even kids, she says. Their parents have probably told them not to get involved with me, not to go near me or provoke me. Who knows whom I'll accuse next, and what I'll claim they did?

From time to time, I get the feeling that Doctor Atwood wishes that this hadn't become a whole legal mess. She'd prefer it if she could just deal with me and my problems without the added pressure of Cynthia trying to set a new *precedent* that might put her in the news and in all the law books.

No one jingles coins at me anymore, in return for which I don't keep wanting to back every kid in the school against the wall and say, "I didn't do it!" Mostly I try not to think about the guys saying I wanted to let other guys grope me for money, but when I do, it still has the power to make me mad, and ashamed, but especially mad—enough so that I've stopped trying to sort through my memory of whether or not Shakes was holding my wrists.

I sort of remember it happened, just as I sort of remember it didn't. But who cares? Something happened. And whatever happened was enough to ruin my life. Every day, the incident itself gets more distant.

Hour by hour, it recedes into the past and gets harder to remember. And who wants to remember, really?

But no matter how much I forget, or *try* to forget, I can't forget the part about them saying I was willing to let guys feel me up for a small fee. That little detail seems to have a life of its own, and it doesn't seem to be losing its power to come around and bite me. Whenever I think about that, I notice that I tend to do something weird. Like, I'll suddenly shout some nonsense word out loud, or I'll run and look in the mirror to see if I look like the kind of person who would do something like that.

One evening, Joan comes home from the office totally wired, and even though she's usually annoyingly anti-TV, she turns on the evening news. Josh and I watch her go through the networks until she finds what she's looking for: courtroom footage of a case in which four hunky guys from some rich Detroit suburb are being accused of raping a retarded girl in their school.

Joan says, "They're throwing the book at these guys." She's so jacked up, she can hardly breathe.

The camera focuses on the boys, who slump down in their seats and look sullen and macho and terrified in their neat haircuts and the brand-new suits that their moms probably bought to make them seem like clean, upstanding, decent citizens. I almost feel sorry for them until I remember what they may, or may not, have done.

"Everything like this that happens is good for us," says Joan. "Good for our side. I mean, not for that poor girl. But it alerts the public consciousness to these cases, and it makes people want to nip this sort of thing in the bud. To pay serious attention to cases like yours, Maisie. It makes people want to take action before things get drastic."

I nearly say that what happened to me wasn't exactly drastic.

Joan says, "Of course, what happened to you wasn't as bad as what happened to that poor unfortunate girl. Heaven knows, it was bad enough. But at least it wasn't rape."

Oops. Joan claps her hand over her mouth and wheels on Josh. I can see her wondering: Does Josh Darling know what a rape *is*? I want to tell Joan that Darling Josh knows the fine points of how you get a girl to take off her T-shirt in front of two hundred sweaty, screaming frat boys.

Josh shrugs, like he doesn't care, like he doesn't know a thing.

"It's our culture," Joan says. "It's the world you kids live in."

Another weird thing is, my grades have improved. My teachers are surprised. I know that, in these situations, victims—which Joan and Cynthia keep telling me that I am—tend to let things slide. They fail their courses and overeat and forget to wash their hair. But I'm not doing any of that, so maybe that means I'm not a victim.

Believe it or not, I've begun to think about college. I know it's years in the future—three and a half years, to be exact—but still, the thought's entered my mind. I think that even if the worst happens—if Joan and Cynthia totally blow this thing and I don't get to go to a different high school and I'm condemned to the unbelievable living hell of staying where I am until I graduate, and it never gets any better, no one ever forgets—even then, I'm going to graduate. I can leave, get out of here, go away to college, and start over somewhere else.

The other thing that's boosted my grades is that now I have all the time in the world for homework. I have nothing *but* time for homework. No long bus rides, no emails or phone calls, no one caring if I'm alive or dead except maybe to think that the whole school would be better off if I weren't around.

I guess I could probably find some chat room frequented by girls who'd been involved in inappropriate groping incidents in the back of *their* school buses. But it would be *really* pathetic to have that be my little club. My own little demographic.

Doctor Atwood keeps telling me that I should try reaching out to other kids—that I should try making friends, maybe even with some of the girls in my class. Maybe they have sympathy for me, and they're just hesitant to express it. Maybe something similar happened to them. Plenty of girls have been in situations in which they haven't felt in control of what happens to them and their bodies.

Every time she says it, I have one of those moments of thinking she doesn't know *anything* about people. She has no idea what she's talking about. Because the girls in my school think they *are* the boys, or they want to *be* the boys. They're totally identified with the boys. The boys are kings, they're gods. And no girl is going to be friends with a girl who represents the most pitiful kind of loser a girl can be. And that loser girl would be me.

Besides, it's not exactly something you can go around asking people. *Excuse me, but did you ever have anybody touch your boobs when you didn't want them to? Really? Wanna be friends?*

Though I would never admit it to anyone—so maybe it's good that there's no one I could admit it to, even if I *did* want to—I'm actually starting to like doing homework. How pathetic is *that*? Math is still boring and hard, but sometimes, when I'm working on an assignment or paper or book report for English or social studies, and I'm at my computer, writing it over and over until it's as perfect as I can make it, I suddenly notice that hours have gone by—hours in which I haven't thought once about Shakes and Chris and Kevin.

We've been studying the Bill of Rights, and I like knowing about it. I like knowing what my rights are, and what the people who started this country went through to make sure I had those rights, and that they couldn't be taken away from me. I'd read *Huckleberry Finn* when I was in Wisconsin, but this time, reading it for school, I get really caught up in Huck's whole thing about lying and telling the truth and how you can tell one from the other, and if there are times when it might even be okay to lie.

Our English teacher is always talking about how characters in books learn through suffering, so maybe that's what's happening to me. Sometimes, in the evenings, I turn on the news—not just to find out about rape trials, like Joan does, but to learn what's going on in the world. And when I see people who are poor, or who have just lost someone in their family, or who are in the middle of a war raging around them—well, I don't know how to explain it, but I just feel *sorrier* for them than I ever did before.

Maybe it makes me seem really self-centered, but the truth is, I think about people like that when I start feeling sorry for myself. I won't say that it cheers me up, but it puts things in perspective. I mean, let's face it. Having some guys—your former best friends—touch your breasts isn't the worst thing that ever happened to anybody in the world.

Still, it's pretty bad. I'd be lying if I didn't say things got really lonely, with no friends and no one to talk to except my therapist and my lawyer and my parents. It's made me appreciate Darling Josh. He's an intelligent, sensible little kid. Once, he asked me if it was true that I'd be going away to boarding school pretty soon. I told him I hoped so, and then I felt bad because it was as if I was saying I hoped I'd leave *him*.

So I said, "I'd just like to go somewhere where the kids are a little . . . cooler. A little nicer. Know what I mean?"

And Josh said, "I do know what you mean."

Meanwhile, days go by. A week, then another week. I keep thinking winter is just about to end, and then it turns out to have another giant snowstorm up its cold white sleeve.

Sometimes the phone rings, and I listen to Joan's half of the argument she's been having with my real mom about my going back to Wisconsin. I know Mom thinks I should get away from the nightmare that school has become.

One evening, I creep into the next room to eavesdrop. I mean, after all, they're talking about *me*. It's my future they're discussing. Not that it would occur to them to consult me. It's like it's *their* decision, though I know that, in the end, they won't force me to go anywhere I don't want to go. Like Wisconsin, for example.

I hide behind the door just in time to hear Joan say, "You know, Jeanette, I think that standing up for her rights—her rights as a woman—may be the most important part of any education Maisie will ever get. If we win, which believe me, we *will*, this lesson will stay with her for a lifetime."

It cheers me up to imagine the expression that must be on my mom's face as she listens to Joan. By now, my mother's eyes must be flipped all the way back in her head.

Joan says, "It will make her the kind of woman that I wish we all were. How can you deny her that, and how do you think it will look for Cynthia and me to go through all this, and then have her turn and run?"

Wicked Witch, I think. For a minute I'm almost tempted to go and live with my mom just so it *will* look bad for Joan. But then I remember Geoff and the TV remote. Also, I want to stick around and see how things are going to turn out. So I creep away from my hiding place without letting Joan know I've heard.

When Mom gets me on the phone, she says, "You don't have to stay there. There's no need for you to suffer through this. They can have the hearing or trial or whatever circus they're planning. They can make their point, or whatever Joan's doing for the greater glory of Joan, without dragging you through this."

I know my mom must feel pretty strongly, because she and Dad seem to have made a sort of pact not to criticize the other person or the other person's new spouse. It surprises me that she's breaking their agreement, which she never does.

I say, "I want to be here, Mom."

I guess I must sound so definite, she doesn't bother asking me why. Which is lucky for me, because I couldn't really tell her if she asked.

CHAPTER EIGHTEEN

Anything can start to seem routine. My awful life has begun to seem normal. There's a kind of order to it, it's almost comfortingly familiar: solitude and homework and trying not to think about what everyone thinks about me.

I still see Doctor Atwood twice a week. For most of the hour she listens to me complain. I know she feels sorry for me, and I don't ever think that she's rushing me to get over this whole thing, to get over myself. To move on. But one thing she *does* say is that I need to stop feeling quite so self-conscious. Because I just might be wrong when I think that the other kids are thinking about nothing—and no one—but me.

"I *don't* think that," I say one day. "I just think that when they *do* think about me, they think about what happened on the bus."

"Maybe they don't think about you at all," Doctor Atwood says. "Teenagers have short attention spans. They're probably thinking about their parents, their girlfriends and boyfriends, they're thinking about a million things before they even get to the subject of you."

"Am I being a narcissist?" I smile at her.

"Not exactly," she says. "Even paranoids have enemies."

"What does that mean?" I ask her.

"Let's talk about it another time," she says. "I'm just suggesting it might help you feel better to tell yourself that you're not at the center of everyone's consciousness."

In fact, that makes me feel worse. It's bad enough

that none of the kids talk to me, or look at me. If they don't even think of me, how do I know I exist?

A funny thing: Around this time, there's a school essay-writing contest about the line "I think, therefore I am." I spend a long time thinking about it, and working on it. I really try to wrestle with the question of whether I am because I think I am. Or whether I am because other people think I am.

It's infuriating that Daria Wells wins. She gets to read her essay aloud in front of the whole assembly. It's all about how happy she is to live in a country where she's free to think whatever she likes. Then the whole essay turns into one big boast about how much thinking she does and how much she loves to watch her brilliant mind flitting like a butterfly from one fascinating subject to another. "Like a butterfly!" She actually wrote that! When what she should have written was, "I run to the principal and tell on other kids, therefore I am."

Of course, I wasn't ever going to win any prizes, no matter how brilliant my essay was. Everyone knows who I am, and no one's going to let Hester Prynne stand up and read *her* essay in front of the whole school.

One evening, I walk into the kitchen to find Joan making some disgusting casserole she tells me she read about in a magazine.

She says, "You won't believe it, Maisie, but a single helping of this contains all the minerals and vitamins that our family needs for an entire day."

It's supposed to be lasagna, but it's all green and chewed-up looking. In fact, it's the color of the gunk that's been growing around the bathtub faucet in my bathroom, where Joan hardly ever goes.

I know I should probably go to my room before I say something nasty about Joan's supernutritious, gross cuisine. But I stick around to watch the spectacle of Joan misplacing her knife and finding it again, chopping everything way too small, nicking her finger, bleeding into the food, finding a Band-Aid, adding too much salt and pepper. All the time, I know that she's thinking of herself as some celebrity chef on TV. It's the *Cooking with Joan* show, and Joan's showing her loyal viewers and devoted fans how to stuff their families with so many vitamins, they'll never need to eat again. They'll never *want* to eat again.

"Get the phone, will you, dear?" she says, holding up her nasty green hands.

Cynthia says, "How are you, Maisie?"

"Fine," I say.

"Can I speak to Joan?" At least she doesn't call her *your mom*.

Joan makes motions that force me to hold the phone to her ear. I hate the way her stiff hair feels as it brushes against my wrist.

Whatever Cynthia's calling about must be pretty important, because Joan says, "Wait a second. Wait a second." She goes and washes off her hands so she can actually hold the phone herself.

"Tell me again."

When Joan finally hangs up, she's delirious with joy. It turns out that there *is* going to be some preliminary something or other in front of some civil court judge. It's scheduled for three weeks from now.

"At least we're making progress," says Joan.

I say, "That's good. I guess."

"Of course it's good," Joan says.

"When do they depose me?" I say.

"Listen to you," says Joan. "Depose. A whole new vocabulary. How amazing. I know it's been tough for you, Maisie. But it has been a real education in the legal system and about the rights that you have as a citizen and a woman."

"Thanks," I say. "That must mean it's good that it happened, I guess."

"I don't mean that," says Joan.

"So when is it?" I say.

"When is what?" She's going to make me say it.

"The deposition."

"The deposition's next week."

"Who's going to be there?"

"No one, honey. You, me, Cynthia. And a tape recorder."

So now I'm obsessed with the tape recorder. I think about it all the time.

In my fantasy, I keep getting to the part of the story where I'm talking about saying *no* and Shakes is holding my wrists. Then I imagine myself stopping in the middle of a sentence and saying, "Or anyway, that's how

I *think* it happened. I'm not all that sure."

Think won't be good enough. *Think* won't exactly cut it for Cynthia or Joan. And that will be the end of that. No new school, no money, no making Shakes and Kevin and Chris see that you don't go around saying that a person asked you to find someone to pay her to touch her boobs, just because that person *has* boobs, and because she used to be your friend, and because she chose one of you over the other two.

Every moment when I'm not busy and doing something, like, for example, when I'm trying to fall asleep—not that I *can* sleep—I go over my speech in my head. I rehearse every word of the deposition I'm going to give. The story of how I said *no*, and of how Shakes held my hands, and of how they kept touching me and touching me, and of how I was so scared that I pretended that it felt good. I even said it out loud.

By now, it's a miracle that I can do anything else. Walking to Doctor Atwood's, I used to think about what I was going to say to her. But now all that seems unreal, and the only real thing is what I'm going to say on the tape.

Pretty soon, the scene in the lawyer's office—the scene that hasn't happened yet—is more real to me than anything that *has* happened. Everything looks like a double exposure, like one of those photos where they've screwed up in the lab and two images get printed, one over the other. The image of the present moment always seems to be stamped beneath the scene of myself talking into Cynthia's tape recorder.

"Maisie," Doctor Atwood says one afternoon. "You're a million miles away. Want to talk about what's bothering you?"

What's bothering me? She knows the deposition is only a few days away. What does she *think* is bothering me?

"I was just thinking," I say.

"About what?" she says.

"Next week is the deposition." Might as well point out the obvious, since she doesn't seem to be getting it. I've figured out that one of her techniques is to make me say stuff out loud, even if she already knows it.

"Are you nervous about it?"

Did she really just ask me that?

"No. I mean yes."

"What do you imagine that makes you nervous?"

I close my eyes and try to get into the fantasy, which isn't all that hard, since it's always right there, right alongside what's really happening.

"The tape recorder's going," I say. "Some legal secretary says the date and the place and explains that it's me, Maisie, and that I'm going to give my statement. I open my mouth and start to talk, but I can't get anything to make sense. I start making excuses. I say it's been so long since the incident on the bus, I'm not really sure what I remember and what happened and what I think happened. And I go on talking and talking, sounding more and more spacey and brain-damaged, digging myself in deeper, until everybody's looking at me like it is *The Crucible*. Like I've made the whole thing up just to get attention or maybe because I *am* some kind of sexually weird hysteric, which means I probably *did* ask them to find someone who'd pay to touch my boobs."

"But you know that didn't happen, don't you?"

I nod.

"And you know what *did* happen?"

"I guess so."

"Stay with that, Maisie. What do you mean, you guess so?"

I'm quiet for a while. Then I hear it—the voice of my deliverance. Phlegm Man hacking and coughing in the next room.

"The hour's up," I say.

"Do you want to schedule another session this week?" she asks. "It's not something I usually do. But when a patient's clearly in crisis . . ."

"I'm not in crisis." I hate the word *crisis*. I don't even like the word *patient*. "I'm fine. I'll be fine. Trust me. I'll be fine."

CHAPTER NINETEEN

Two days before I'm supposed to make my statement, my *deposition*, I'm in English class, and someone knocks on the door. It's Diane, one of the secretaries who works in the front office. Somehow I know that it's about me, and as she whispers to the teacher and scans the room, I know she's looking for me.

I'm right. It turns out that I need to go to the principal's office, right away. I wonder what new horror is waiting for me. What have I done now?

On the way, I ask Diane if she knows what this is about.

"I don't think it's anything serious," she says, but something in her tone makes me doubt her. Halfway there, I realize that this is the first time I've been to Doctor Nyswander's office since the day they told me that everyone believed I'd practically begged the guys to touch my boobs and asked them to find guys who'd pay me so someone could do it some more.

No wonder I'm nervous! That is, even more nervous than I usually am these days, which is pretty nervous. Red alert. In fact, I feel like I'm revisiting the scene of some disaster or traumatic accident—the curve where the car ran off the road, the place where my house used to be before the tornado destroyed it. As I get nearer to the office, I'm literally shaking. I practically have to put my fingers over my eyes, like at a slasher movie, before I can look in the general direction of Doctor Nyswander's door. But he's got the door closed. He's probably telling some other poor kid something that's going to ruin *her* life.

"Maisie," says Joy, the principal's secretary. "What's wrong? You look pale."

What's wrong is that Joy knows my name, as if I'm some kind of school celebrity. But of course they know who I am. I'm the one who's suing the school board. Still, even at the height of my paranoia, it doesn't seem like they're looking at me as if I'm their enemy. In fact, they look worried, sympathetic. Of course. That makes sense, too. I'm the poor victim-girl who got molested in the back of the school bus.

"Am I in trouble?" It takes all my concentration to get those four words out, and somehow it calms me down. "I mean, *more* trouble?"

"Why would you think that?" asks Joy.

I think, *Because I am?* "Then why am I here?"

"Oh." Joy actually has to think a minute. "That's right. Your stepmom called. Her car broke down, so she can't pick you up this afternoon. She needs you to take the school bus home. She'll meet you back at the house."

Joan's fancy Volvo broke down? For some reason, this makes me so happy that I have to fight the urge to high-five Joy and Diane. I imagine the look on Joan's face when her dream vehicle wouldn't start. I imagine all sorts of grisly automotive scenes: smoke pouring out from under the hood, the brakes locking on a downhill curve. I can practically hear the sounds of the engine sputtering and dying, sputtering and dying.

Then I say, "I don't get it. Why did I have to come all the way here? Why couldn't you just send a note to the teacher to give to me? That's what happens when other kids' parents need to get them a message, right?" I'm wondering if Joan is such royalty around here that her needs and requests get special treatment.

Joy and Diane exchange quick looks, and suddenly I understand. Joan probably started yelling at them before she even said hello. I imagine her saying something like, "Given the efficiency with which you people have handled problems in the past, I want a personal guarantee—I want witnesses!—that my stepdaughter will get the message." I understand that they're scared of Joan, afraid she'll sue them about this, too. And maybe that's why they look so sorry for me. It's not just because I'm the girl to whom that *thing* happened on the bus, it's because I'm the poor victim who has to live with Joan.

The whole situation must be making me stupider, slower to react. Because only now do I think, *The bus. I'm going to have to take the bus home from school.*

Doctor Atwood has told me not to dwell on the thoughts that I know are going to make me miserable. So here's a thought I try not to have. Or if I think it once, I try not to think it twice. In a row. Ever since the incident, I've sort of felt like I was dead. Or, to be more exact, I feel like that girl in *Our Town*, the play the seniors put on last year. I feel like the girl, Emily, in that scene where she looks at the world from heaven. Or like those characters in movies where the person dies and then gets a chance to come back to earth and see life going merrily on without them.

I've been feeling as if there used to be the living Maisie who used to go to school and hang out with her friends and ride the bus and whatever. And now there is the other me who might as well be in another world, haunting the places where that other Maisie used to live. Sometimes I close my eyes when I see the school buses parked in front of the school, or when any bright yellow vehicle passes us on the road. Because that's when it really gets painful, when I compare my old life with the life I have now, and I think, *I used to ride a bus just like that, like a regular ninth grader.*

The three o'clock bell rings and, as always, the whole school erupts. You'd never think the same thing happens at the end of every day. You'd think the bell had never rung before, that the kids had been stuck at school forever. Everybody's so happy to be set free. Everybody, that is, but me.

It seems amazing that my old bus—number 29—is parked in the same place where it always used to be on the afternoons when I used to take it. I hang back and wait till the other kids have gotten on, because I don't want to be sitting there and have to look at them, one by one, as they board and walk past me. Then I realize I've made a mistake, because I could have sat down and buried my face in a book and refused to look up. But now they'll all be looking up at *me*, and there will be no way to avoid them as I try to find an empty seat, or look around for someone who's brave or stupid enough to agree to sit next to Leprosy Girl.

As I get on, Big Maureen says, "Hi, Maisie. Haven't seen *you* in a while."

"Hi." I glare at her. Why did she have to open her mouth and say anything at all? She never talked to me before, when I used to ride her stupid bus every day. Maybe she's trying to make me feel comfortable, or maybe she just thought it would be weird not to say anything, not to acknowledge that there was a problem. Or maybe she feels guilty because the incident happened on her bus.

I think she's trying to be nice. Okay, I *know* she's trying to be nice. But the truth is, I'd like to kill her, or at least tell her to shut up. But of course I don't. She's already shut up. And maybe I'm being rewarded for not being rude to Big Maureen, because sure enough there's an empty seat directly behind her. It's the perfect place to hide.

I don't look at one single kid, and I don't want anyone to look at me. I feel like, if I make eye contact with another human being, I'll melt, like the witch in *The Wizard of Oz*.

I grab the seat and sit right near the edge on the

aisle, so someone would have to tell me to move over if they want to sit down. Which they won't, because it's me. No one's going to sit next to me. On the one-in-a-million chance that someone doesn't know who I am, that person won't be able to ask me to move over, because I'll be reading.

I grab a book from my backpack and open it at random and pretend to read before I even know what book it is. It's my American history textbook, and I've turned to the part about the Civil War, which we've just studied. I read about slavery for a while. I feel like it's a message. A private communication that says, *Maisie, get over yourself!* Human beings were being bought and sold and whipped and separated from their families, and *you're* worried about riding a bus you haven't been on since some kids touched your boobs?

I take a deep breath and find my actual homework assignment. It's a chapter about the Spanish-American War. The motor starts up, and we pull away from school. So far, so good, I'm okay.

I read about how President Theodore Roosevelt said, "Speak softly and carry a big stick." It's something

I need to remember, partly because it's the sort of thing that could definitely be on a test, and partly because it sounds like good advice. Or is it? If you carry a big stick, does that mean you'll have to hit someone with it? Or that you'll never have to hit someone with it, because they'll see the big stick and leave you alone?

I'm so busy fishing around in my backpack, trying to find my highlighting pen, that it takes me a while to hear a voice and realize that someone is talking to me.

The voice says, "Can I sit down?"

It can't be talking to me. I don't even bother to look up, but the voice repeats the same question again until I have no choice.

I look up. It's Shakes. He's looking at me. All sorts of twisty, Shakes-like expressions are working their way across his face. If it were anyone else, I'd think he was trying to figure out whether it was okay to smile or not, but with Shakes, it's hard to be sure.

First I think I'm going to faint. Then I think, You can't faint when you're sitting down. Then I think, How do they *know* you can't? In the history of the world, it's probably happened at least once that a sitting person fainted. Then I stop thinking, and just try to deal with the blood rushing back and forth between my ears and the fact that my stomach is flipping over and over.

No, I think. *You* can't *sit down. Not after what you did.*

The bus starts up, and Shakes grins at me. Without either of us having to say so, we both know that the other's thinking about that morning when Shakes went flying all over the school bus so the seniors would let him sit in back. It seems like it happened a million years ago.

"Sure," I say. And now I actually smile and move over. I can't believe I'm smiling! After what he did! I mean, who *is* this guy? Who was he? Who did I *think* he was?

It doesn't help to remember those mornings on the bus when it was just Shakes and me. That's the part I can't stand to think about, the part of my other life. What did I think we were doing? And what could *he* have thought?

"Might as well sit down," I say. "You're going to hurt yourself, standing like that."

In our old lives, I would never have said that. No one

was allowed to mention the fact that Shakes has physical problems unless he himself used his disability to get his way, like with the seniors. But now it's almost as if I *want* to hurt his feelings. After what he did . . . but what makes it harder is that I can tell Shakes understands all that, he understands why I said it. That's how well we know each other. How well we still know each other.

He sits, and I slide over even more so I'm as far from him as possible, and we're not touching.

"How are you?" asks Shakes.

"Just great," I say. "Thanks for asking. And you?" When I was really little, I used to be so scared of talking in class, it practically made me throw up. And this is worse. Just getting the words out leaves me winded and weak in the knees. Maybe you *can* faint sitting down—

"Not so great," Shakes says.

I wonder if he's been sick, missing school. For a moment, I'm so concerned that I forget how mad I am at him, and I look at him, like I used to, to see how he is. He looks pale, and tired. He's got dark circles under his eyes.

"Have you been sick?" I say, looking hard at him.

He stares back at me. We were never supposed to talk about this. But then again, he was never supposed to tell the other guys that I let him touch me.

"No more than usual," he says.

"Then what's your problem?"

"What makes you think I have a problem?"

"You look like crap," I say.

The silence that falls is long enough to give me plenty of time to feel sorry for having said that. But why should I feel sorry after what he did to me?

"I miss you," Shakes says.

I'm sure I must have heard him wrong. But I can't exactly ask him to say it again. I try to think of all the things he *could* have been saying, and probably *was* saying, all the phrases that might sound like "I miss you." But when I can't think of anything, I wind up feeling pretty sure that's what he said.

Suddenly, he twitches so violently that his hand flies out and pokes me in the ribs.

"Hey, watch it!" I say.

If I hadn't been wearing my puffy jacket, he could actually have hurt me. It's the worst spasm I've ever seen him have, and I wonder if he's nervous around me, and if that's making his twitching worse. For a moment I'm almost glad. It serves him right. Then I stop being glad. I don't want him to get any worse. It makes me realize I'm really not as mad at him as I'd thought, or maybe I just like him more than I'd let myself remember.

"I'm sorry, Maisie," he says.

I can't tell if he means sorry for accidentally hitting me, or sorry for telling people that I'd let him touch me, or both.

He says, "I liked it better when we were friends."

I say, "You should have thought of that. You should have thought of that before you told Kevin and Chris what we were doing, those mornings, in the back of the bus. You should have thought of that before you let them ask me if they could do it, too. You should have thought of that before you didn't stick up for me. You should have thought of that before you just rolled over when Daria told the principal. You should have thought of that—" I don't know whether I'm actually going to be able to say this part. I take a deep breath and say, "You should have thought of that before you told everybody that I asked you if there were guys who would pay to touch my boobs."

"I didn't," says Shakes. "I never did. I don't know what came over me. I was freaked out, I wasn't thinking when I let them do it, and I didn't protect you. But I promise, I never did."

"Never did what?" I say.

"I never said that part about the money. That was all Kevin and Chris's idea. I don't even know where they got that from. They just decided to say that, if someone told, and from the look on Daria's face that morning, that seemed like a done deal. If we got in trouble, they decided we would say that, and that we would make it seem like the whole thing was your idea. I was against it from the start. I couldn't believe they'd actually go through with it. I knew how terrible you would feel if you ever found out."

"Found out? I found out the next day! Were you around—were you *alive*—when all those kids were jingling coins in their pockets and they drew that . . . thing on the girls' bathroom wall?"

"I don't go in the girl's bathroom," says Shakes.

"But you knew I was going to find out."

"I guess so. But I didn't say it. I never said that thing about the money."

"You swear?"

"I swear. You've got to believe me. I never said it."

I look at Shakes even harder now. And the weird thing is, I *do* believe him. I've known him since pre-school, I know him almost as well as I know myself. I can tell when he's lying and telling the truth. But there's this: If I can't be sure about what really happened to *me*, how can Shakes be so sure? Maybe he *thinks* he's telling the truth. For all I know, he was the one who came up with the idea to add the part about the money. But somehow I doubt it. I doubt it.

I say, "Did you tell anyone it *wasn't* true?"

"No," he says. "I'm sorry. I already told you I was sorry."

"If you didn't deny it, if you didn't stick up for me, you might as well have said it *was* true."

"It wasn't like that," he says. "Everything was happening so fast, and all these faces and voices and weirdness were all sort of swirling around, and everybody got very panicky and crazy even though the principal was trying to be all reasonable and supercalm. I could see him sweating under his tie."

"I know," I say. "He does that."

"I didn't really get a chance to say what was true and what wasn't. Everyone was sort of rushing from one thing to the next. It was like they were skipping from rock to rock in a stream."

I remember when we did that. He *wants* me to remember. I want to say, *Bringing that up isn't fair!* But how would I answer if he asked me why?

I say, "Not saying it's a lie is pretty much the same as saying something's true."

"It isn't. Not exactly. Don't be so harsh, Maisie."

"I'm not," I say. "And you know I'm right."

"Then what about the lie *you* told about how I held your hands down while it was happening and wouldn't let you move? I heard about that from my mom. You know *that* isn't true. You know that never happened."

"It *is* true," I say. But I'm thinking, *It isn't? Is it?*

It's so confusing—and painful, I guess—that, all at once, we both simultaneously run out of energy. We run out of things to say. After that we just sit there side by side on the bus seat, staring at each other. We're both a little winded, as if we've run a long race—a marathon. Then we slump back against the seat, and our heads drift together until we're leaning against each other.

It feels nice. Really nice. At the same time I can feel the whole bus looking at us. Behind us, everyone's eyes are drilling into the backs of our skulls. I wonder where Kevin and Chris are, but I don't care, it feels so good. It's almost as if we've magically time-traveled back to that other time, that period of grace when I didn't even know enough to appreciate what we had. We're back where we belong. Beside each other. Together.

I think about all the time I've spent in the bad world of thinking that Shakes didn't care about me or that he hated me or that he'd told all those lies about me. And now I feel that I've come back from a long, hard journey. I've returned to the good world where it's just me and Shakes.

Sitting there with our eyes closed and our heads pressed together, I'm half blissing out on the moment and half trying to figure out—just in case a moment like this doesn't ever come again—what Shakes and I had.

Or what we *have*, what we mean to each other. Were we in love? Did we have crushes on each other? Did we find each other exactly when we needed someone? We were friends, there was that. What do I know? Maybe it had nothing, or hardly anything, to do with the fact that I have breasts.

The truth is, I don't think I'll ever be able to forgive Shakes for not defending me. For not realizing that you just can't say certain things, or allow certain things to be said about people. Especially your friends. I guess I'll never forgive him for not being braver and more independent. Those are qualities you care about in a person—maybe even more than that person's ability to get over his physical problems. Shakes was pretty brave, but not brave enough, when the going got really tough. And the truth was, I guess I hadn't been all that brave or independent, either.

I don't want to think about that now. For the moment, I'm comfortable, and almost happy. I feel relaxed and sleepy—for the first time in a long while. But I know better than to doze off. We're not alone on the bus. Everything we do or don't do is a statement. It has meaning. We can't pretend that the rest of the world doesn't exist. It's right there with us in all those rows behind us.

It makes me sad to realize that by the time I get home, I'll have decided that no matter how much I like Shakes, no matter how good it feels to be leaning against him, the closeness between us can't go on. It's too late for us to be friends. I'll never trust him the way I used to. We'll be nice to each other when we see each other in school, but we're no longer the same people we used to be. And it's sad, because, whatever happened, he was my oldest friend.

I remember something Doctor Atwood said. "It's unfortunate," she said, "and no one likes it. But friendships die all the time. And other friendships are born."

Shakes's sigh rattles his scarecrow body. He says, "I meant it about being sorry. But you can do whatever you want. Get us expelled. We probably deserve it. I don't care. I just wanted to sit next to you one more time."

I say, "I appreciate that. I mean it, Shakes. I really do."

"Well, good," says Shakes. "I always really liked you."

"I liked you, too. I still do. Just not the same way."

"I understand that," says Shakes. "I don't blame you."

"I'm sorry," I say.

"No," Shakes says. "I'm the one who's sorry."

"I accept your apology," I say.

But I don't. I can't. Not yet.

Meanwhile, I can't help wondering if Shakes, like me, couldn't really remember if he'd done it or not. Because the part that's a lie—that I'd said *no* and that Shakes held down my hands—had begun to seem more like the truth every time I told it.

I'm crying a little when Shakes gets off the bus, so I pretend to be looking out the window as I mumble, "Okay. See you later." I'm thinking that I've got another ten minutes till I get to my house, so by then I'll have a little time to think things through and decide how I feel about what's just happened between me and Shakes. But in fact I spend those minutes trying *not* to think. I'm not ready to deal with it yet. Or at all. And I need more time. After everything that's happened, ten minutes seems like nothing.

Outside, the snow has shrunk to dirty white patches.

The lawns are a muddy brown. Here and there, a greenish fuzz is sprouting after all those months of waiting under the snow. I feel as if I'm trying to memorize every spot we pass, every turn in the road, because soon this minute will be gone, replaced by other minutes. And by the next time I come back this way, everything will be different. It will never again look the way it did on the day Shakes told me he was sorry and that he still liked me, and I told him that wasn't good enough. It all seems too sad for words, especially since I can't believe that my life will ever get any better than it is at this moment.

I tiptoe into my house, shutting the door so softly that you'd need superhuman powers to hear. Which Joan has, obviously.

"Maisie," she calls from the kitchen. "Come in here for a minute. I've made something special I want to show you."

I walk in as slowly as I can, putting off the moment of seeing whatever gourmet gross-out Sitcom Mom has prepared for my delight. It turns out to be a chocolate cake.

"Get it?" asks Joan.

Ten minutes ago I was sitting with my head against Shakes's head. And now I'm in the kitchen with Joan trying to figure out what I'm supposed to "get" about a cake.

"Get what?" I say. "It's a cake."

"No," says Joan. "It's a law book. Like the kind Cynthia has in her office."

It hits me that, in Joan's insane misguided mind, the cake is supposed to be some kind of celebration-in-advance, for when I give my deposition in Cynthia's office, surrounded by books that look pretty much like giant chocolate blobs and are no less fake than a book made of cake. By this time tomorrow, my hour at Cynthia's will be over, and the case will be ready for the hearing. And Joan's sure we'll win! Hooray! Let's celebrate! Law-book cake for everybody!

"Cool," I say. "Can I go now?"

"Maisie! Maisie! What's wrong? What happened to you at school today? You look like you've seen a ghost! Was the bus ride home sheer hell for you? I can't tell you how sorry I am. Short of dragging that darn piece-of-garbage SUV to the dealership myself, there's no way

I could have gotten there in time. And of course your dad insisted on buying me something so fancy and foreign that the nearest dealership is forty miles away. I had to wait for them to get here and bring me a loaner. It ruined my entire day."

"Did you get the car fixed?" I ask. Joan smiles. Even thought it's broken, she'd still rather talk about her car than about whatever problems I might have been having at school.

"They think there's some computer glitch, which isn't supposed to happen. But no one can be sure, I mean, no carmaker can play God, right? They can do what they can do, but there's a limit!"

"I guess," I say.

"And no matter what kind of fortune you pay—"

"Stuff happens," I say.

"Exactly," says Joan. "So how was the bus ride? Traumatic? Tell me it wasn't so bad. Oh, you poor sweetheart!""

"It was okay, I guess." I'm never going to tell her how it really was. Even if I wanted to—which I don't—I couldn't explain.

"Good," says Joan. "But believe me, after tomorrow, you'll never have to do anything like that again. Of course, we'll have to be patient—these court cases drag on and on like *Bleak House*. But eventually, and I mean starting tomorrow, this will be settled. It will, I promise. There was just a case, down in South Carolina somewhere. Cynthia was telling me last night. There was a fairly considerable settlement awarded to some poor girl. Boarding school, then college. Medical school, if you want."

"I don't want to go to medical school," I say. "I don't want to be a doctor." Then I say, "Speaking of doctors, do you think I could go see Doctor Atwood this afternoon?"

"It's unusual," says Doctor Joan Marbury, Therapist, snapping to attention and instantly emerging out of Sitcom Mom's head.

"She said I could," I tell Joan. "She said she'd be willing to schedule an emergency appointment."

"Emergency! I knew it! I knew something was wrong. What happened? Something. I know it. It's my fault, because of the car and the bus ride and . . . to say nothing of the fact that the deposition's coming up, and I know it's worrying you, though I've told you a thousand times there's nothing to worry about—"

I say, "It has nothing to do with you." Which is true, but only sort of. If Joan's car hadn't broken down, I wouldn't have taken the bus, I wouldn't have had that talk with Shakes. "I really think I'd like to see Doctor Atwood. *Now*."

"Why, that's wonderful. Not wonderful that something happened to you that's made you want to see Doctor Atwood on an emergency basis. But wonderful that you feel you can trust her, that you *want* to talk to her and work your feelings out with her in a crisis situation."

"It's not a crisis. Can I go see her or not?"

"Why don't you call?" Joan hands the phone to me. Doctor Joan Marbury knows that a kid who sounds like a wreck will have an easier time of persuading a busy shrink to stay late in the office.

"You call." I hand the phone back to Joan. She's going to have to come though for me, at least this once.

She takes the phone into the other room.

When she comes back, she says, "She'll see you at

five. I'll drive you over. Throw some water on your face, dear. Let's leave a little early. You never know how these loaners are going to behave in bad weather."

"The weather's perfectly fine," I say, but Joan doesn't seem to hear.

A few blocks from Doctor Atwood's office, we pass a guy—tall, skinny, ordinary looking. He's standing on the edge of the sidewalk, leaning into the street, and from a block away, I can see he's spitting into the gutter. As we get closer, we watch him retching.

"My God, that's disgusting," Joan says. "Someone should alert the sheriff. That could be a health threat. Or a quality-of-life issue. Have you been reading about that guy who traveled around the world with that super-deadly strain of tuberculosis?"

Then, for just a moment, Joan the Human Being wins out over her other multiple personalities, and says, "That poor man. Do you think he's in some kind of trouble? Sick? Do you think he might need help?"

We slow down, and, as we approach, the guy is still coughing and spitting.

Suddenly, I think, *I'd know those sounds anywhere!*

"Phlegm Man!" I say. It seems like a sign, but I can't tell what it's a sign *of*.

"You *know* that person?" Joan says.

"Sort of. He's a patient of Doctor Atwood's. He does that all the time. That's probably why he goes to her. It's probably some nervous thing."

I can tell that Joan's gone back to thinking of Phlegm Man as a disgusting health threat. But now she doesn't want to say so because the poor fellow is seeking help from someone in her own profession. But she does speed up again, to pass him as quickly as possible. In less than a minute, we're at Doctor Atwood's.

"Thanks. I can walk home," I tell Joan, and jump out of the car. I ring Doctor Atwood's bell and go in.

"Maisie," says Doctor Atwood. "Sit down. Sit down." Then she says, "The tissues are right there by the couch."

I'm crying so hard that for a while I can't even speak.

Finally I say, "Can I have a do-over? I need to tell you what happened. I need to start everything over from scratch."

* * *

The story, the parts of the story, don't come out in order, one thing after another. Nor does it make total sense. But for the first time, with anyone—with Doctor Atwood or Joan or the principal or even myself—I try to say, to *really* describe, *exactly* what I remember.

I start way back, with that day I came home from Wisconsin. I start with that day I went to Shakes's house, and I saw the guys noticing that I had breasts. I start with how, right then, I half knew (even though I didn't want to admit it, really) that things would never be the same. I should probably start from preschool, but I think Doctor Atwood understands. I've probably said enough about that already.

Then I tell her about trying to be friends with the guys over the summer. I tell her about trying to pretend that nothing had changed, and how it didn't ever quite work.

I take a deep breath. Then I begin to talk about those mornings on the bus with Shakes. How first everything was an accident, or seemed like an accident, and then it turned into stuff we were doing on purpose. I'm crying really hard now, because it's so sad. I try to explain how much it meant to me, and how good it felt, and how much I cared about Shakes and how much I thought he cared about me. And maybe he did care about me, but not enough. He cared about his friends more, or anyway, he cared more about looking tough in front of his friends.

That's the part she needs to understand in order to understand how, on that day the others asked to touch me and Shakes didn't stop them, I was so shocked, it was as if everything inside me sort of crumpled and disintegrated. It was as if I'd broken a limb or gotten burned or fallen. That's how much it hurt. I really *was* in shock. I didn't know what I was thinking, let alone what I was saying.

I thought, *Fine. Who cares? Go ahead and touch my boobs, if that's all this is about.* I'd thought Shakes and the other two guys liked me for myself. But if it was all about my breasts, I didn't care about any of it. Let them touch my boobs if that was all they really wanted. Why should I care? What did it mean?

When they asked if they could touch me, I asked for some time to think it over, and then I said, "Okay. Fine. Have fun. Go ahead, touch them as much as you want."

I told myself it was no different from their touching

my arm. But it was. Of course it was. It wasn't as if they were touching my arm. It felt really creepy and it made me hate them, even though they were my friends. Then it made me hate myself, and it made me hate my body more than anything else. It was as if I were watching myself, as if I'd zoomed up to the roof of the bus, from where I was watching them act like morons, like those drunken frat boys on the *Girls Gone Wild* shows. I realized my friends were nothing but boys, they'd never be better or different from that. Even Shakes was getting into it.

"Did Shakes hold your hands down?" asks Doctor Atwood. "Did he keep you from resisting?"

It shocks me back to her office.

"No," I say. "I *didn't* resist. I told them they could go ahead and touch me if that was what they wanted. I don't even know if Shakes was one of the ones who was actually touching me. But it *was* happening, and he was definitely part of it. He was there. He didn't defend me. I hated him as much as the others and finally I hated them all so much that I told them it felt good. I wanted them to hear the hate in my voice. I wanted to be tougher than the kind of girl who would say, 'Stop it, please, boys, stop it.' I wanted to be tougher and braver than that.

"But still, I wasn't going to tell anyone. I wouldn't have told on them. Because even after what happened, they were still my old friends. I didn't want to get them into trouble. And besides, there's a code of honor. Kids don't rat each other out. You just don't do that. And even when Joan got involved and we went to the principal's office, I was ready to tough it out."

"Until . . . ?"

"Until I heard that part about the money. And it suddenly hit me that they could tell that lie about me, that kids who'd been my friends since preschool and who I thought really liked me could invent nasty stuff like that just to save themselves. I was just so *angry*. I began to think I couldn't have let them do it unless someone had been holding my hands. Otherwise, I would have punched them and scratched their eyes out. I knew I must have said no, even though it seemed like I was saying yes. In my heart I *meant* no, even if that's not really what I said. And that's when the story started changing."

"No one said anything about money?" asks Doctor Atwood.

"No!" I say. "Haven't you been listening to one word I've been saying?"

"To *every* word," Doctor Atwood says. "I just want to make sure."

"It's the truth," I say.

Neither of us speaks for a long time. I'm still crying and honking into the tissue and dabbing at my eyes.

"What do you want to do now?" she says. "You don't have to answer right away. Or even today. Take your time. Take as long as you need."

CHAPTER TWENTY

At first I was nervous about telling the truth, especially now that I finally knew what the truth *was*. What would people think of me when they found out I hadn't struggled and resisted, but I'd just caved in and told the guys, "Sure. Go ahead. Whatever." I assumed that everybody was going to come down really hard on me for accusing the boys of molesting me, of touching me against my will, of forcing me to do something as if they didn't know that no means no.

Joan and Cynthia were especially upset, but the weird thing was, they seemed less mad at me for having lied than for having weakened their case by lying and then trying to set things straight. And Joan really got bent out of shape when I told her I was determined that we drop the charges. Maybe she and Cynthia thought they were going to go down in some history books as crusaders for women's rights, or something. The dreaded hearing or trial I'd been dreaming about for so long never took place, and they canceled the deposition in Cynthia's office. Joan still tried to persuade me to go forward with the suit, because apparently it's still an offense to touch a girl's breasts whether she wants you to, or not. No means no, but, as it turns out, yes also means no. Even if I did tell them it was okay, it *wasn't* okay. So everything was still pretty complicated.

For a while the school wanted us—that is, me and my dad and Joan and Chris and Kevin and Shakes and their parents—to all get together for a big meeting. Doctor Nyswander had gotten the idea from something they did in countries where there had been a revolution or a dictatorship, and innocent people had been put in prison or killed. At the meeting, I would talk about what happened, and how I felt about it, and the boys would talk about why they did what they did, and how sorry they were, and everybody would kiss and make up and go home happy. I half wanted it to happen. I would have liked to hear Chris and Kevin admit that they'd ruined our friendship because they were so jealous of me and Shakes, just as I would have liked to hear Shakes admit that when the others made him choose between them and me, he didn't have the courage to choose me. But I knew they were never going to admit any of that, so it was fine with me when enough of the parents objected and the meeting didn't happen. Instead, the boys and I all had to write essays—as punishment, I guess. They had to write on the theme of "Respect." The title of my essay was supposed to be "The Truth Shall Make You Free." I had a hard time with it, because the truth was, even after I'd admitted to lying, I still didn't feel all that liberated. So I just wrote down the first thoughts that popped into my head, and handed the essay in. I don't know if anyone ever actually read it.

Everybody, I mean everybody except Cynthia and

Joan, was happy to see the whole thing go away.

Shakes's mom got married that June, and they moved to Delaware. I was sorry to see him go, but on the other hand, it solved a lot of problems, not having to see him every day. It turned out that Kevin is really good at math, so he got sent away to a special math school in Philadelphia, and I haven't seen him anymore, either. Without Kevin and Shakes around, Chris has turned into just another guy, and I guess I must have turned into just another girl. I was no longer the girl who asked the guys to find kids who'd pay to touch her. Word got out that part hadn't happened. And I think all the kids felt a little ashamed of themselves for being so quick to think it had.

They were supernice to me for a while, and then that stopped, too. After that, I've been just a regular kid, like any other.

I've done well in school since then. That is something that has stayed with me, so maybe I should be grateful to the guys for turning me in that direction.

But I'm not grateful. I never was. I wish it hadn't happened.

But just like Joan kept saying at the time, it was

part of my education. And I learned from it, I did. I'll never again be able to watch TV or read the newspaper and hear someone say such and such a thing is true without remembering those awful months. I still believe that there's such a thing as the truth, and I still try never to lie. And yet I can never forget how certain—and then how uncertain—I was, every time I told and retold the story of how some boys, my former best friends, touched me on the bus.